CW00517643

To

Karina

Always Protect

AA Andrew

Care To Protect

(Caring Hands Series)

By

T.A. Andrews

T.A. Andrews

Care To Protect

Copyright

T.A. Andrews

Care To Protect

Contents

T.A. Andrews

Dedication

To my best friend Vicki

T.A. Andrews

Acknowledgements

It's my first time ever writing acknowledgments, it's kind of scary.

First of all, I have to thank my amazing husband, you've supported me throughout everything. From the first day I came and said I had started writing book, you've encouraged me. I will forever love you for it.

Vicki, without my partner in crime, I wouldn't have been able to do any of this. Love you more than words can say.

My other half of me. She knows who she is, she supports me through everything. Has been there every step of the way and will forever not only be my best friend, but my amazing family.

My naughty corner bosses. You three ladies have not only given me encouragement but you have pushed me to keep going. I love our daily chats and love the friendship we have. You have told me no end of times how proud you are of me and it just makes my heart burst with pride. Through you showing me how amazing you all are, it's given me the strength to be able to do it myself. I love you all from the bottom of my heart and will be forever grateful you all came into my life.

Tracy. From the beginning, you was the one who said I could do it. You said 'never say never' and pushed me on the first day to go for it. Thank you for everything you've done for me, you are honestly one of my best friends and so glad you're in my life.

The amazing authors I know and work with. Along the way you have showed me through your books and words, I could do it. Thank you.

My amazing beta readers, thank you for dropping everything and reading this book for me. Thank you for the advice you gave me. You helped make this story amazing.

My editor, you told me on a few occasions it was a good story when the self-doubt kicked in. Thank you for taking a chance on this new author.

Thank you to everyone who reads this book, I can't wait to give you more of my stories.

Blurb

My life was good, I had my gorgeous daughter and a job I enjoyed. Then he turned up at my door with his captivating eyes and he's about to test my one rule. Never fall for a client, but it's not just us we have to think about, people depend on us.

He wasn't part of my plan, but I can't seem to walk away. I know he wants me, he's more than determined.

I stand by my rules, but as people say. Rules are made to be broken.

Can I make the right choice for us all, and not destroy my career at the same time?

Or will it all come crashing down around us?

T.A. Andrews

Prologue

Lucas

Have you ever stopped to think how your life is? I honestly thought my life was settled, happy and simple. Don't ever think it, your life will turn to shit.

My life was good. I had some great friends; I had a wonderful wife. I loved my job, and now I had my gorgeous little boy. Perfect you might think. Yeah well, what might seem like the perfect family is very far from it.

My life changed after my son was born, well actually more like when my wife found out she was pregnant. Molly didn't want kids so soon. She wanted the life she had already, the nights out, the lunch dates with friends, the spa days. Me, I absolutely couldn't wait to be a dad. When my son came in to the world my heart was fit to burst with love, nothing was going to be too much for him.

I thought Molly would bond once Ben was here, or once she held him. I thought she would instantly fall in love. Well who wouldn't, he was gorgeous? He had my nose, my wife's dimples. The most gorgeous curly little bits of hair on his head, but that was far from how it was. It was me who was up during the night, me who took him for injections and it was me who started his weaning. Molly well, let's put it this way, her lifestyle didn't really change much. She still went on lunch dates with friends, went on her spa days and still went to have her nails done. My love for her grew less and less.

Most evenings were spent arguing. I began to hate the person she had become. My life was hard, juggling work and looking after Ben. Family helped, but I knew I had to get out. I knew I had to make a life on my own with Ben.

My marriage was over, but how could I make it happen?

I had to be strong for Ben, I couldn't fail him.

I wouldn't fail him.

At the end of the day he was all that mattered. I was up for the challenge of being a single dad.

One thing was certain I had to find some stable childcare for Ben, he needed something regular, a routine. I didn't even know where to begin, but I knew I couldn't keep passing him about between people. It isn't fair on him. He may only be ten months old, but that little boy will soon start to be more aware. Its time I sorted my life out.

Chapter One

Charlie

Urgh, Monday morning again. Why the hell do weekends go way too bloody fast? One minute it is Friday evening and then in the next blink it's Monday morning again. Come on, I think we need three-day weekends, but I bet even that wouldn't be long enough. Oh well, best get my arse out this bed. I have some very delightful children turning up at my door very soon, also, Holly is shouting through the baby monitor. She wants breakfast, that girl just doesn't stop eating.

Walking into my daughter's bedroom I see her pulling all her books from the shelf, I knew I should have put them higher.

"Hey baby girl, how was your sleep?" I say picking her up. I swear she weighs more and more each freaking day. For a two-year-old she's not small at all.

"Shall we get ready for the day? Lilly and George will be here very soon for you to play with." Holly just looks at me like she really doesn't care.

"Come on baby girl, you want some breakfast?" Now that gets her attention.

"Chocolate cereal," she says. I moan under my breath, why did I ever introduce her to chocolate cereal?

We go to the bathroom and do our normal routine, then I get us both dressed. We're downstairs by six-fifty am, that gives me ten minutes before the first lot of children arrive.... Oh yeah, did I not say? I'm a childminder. I started this job not long after Holly was born.

Being a single mum, I knew I wouldn't be able to leave her, but I wanted to earn my own money and what's better than childminding? I love the job; it's so rewarding seeing the children in my care grow up and become amazing children. Don't get me wrong, there are times when I think, what the hell am I doing this for? That's normally when I have parents moaning about this and that. Or Ofsted; the Office for Standards in Education, Children's Services and Skills, they come and inspect me on a regular basis and drive me insane. It can be such a lonely job, with only children to talk to, making me realise I need more friends.

I'm busy making sure everything is in place when the doorbell goes. That will be Lilly, she's always, without a doubt, on time. Opening the door, I'm greeted with her smiling face.

"Hey beautiful girl." Lilly runs into the porch and hugs my waist tight. "You had a good weekend?" I ask her.

"Yes, we went swimming." Looking at her mum to confirm, she nods.

"Wow bet that was fun for you Lilly. Did you practice what you've learnt?" I ask her.

Lilly nods and then turns to hang her coat and book bag on her peg. Lilly is four-years-old and hasn't been at school long, she's still in reception class, but she is loving it.

After taking her shoes off and saying goodbye to mum, we both head into the playroom where Holly is. In the five minutes I have been at the door she's already trashed the room.

"Oh, bloody hell," I mumble under my breath, so the kids can't hear me. I can see how today, and this week is going to go, if I am already tidying a trashed room and it's not even eight am. I start to tidy up when the doorbell goes again. This is what it is like every morning, Piccadilly Circus. Going to the door I see George staring through the window, grinning at me, I can't help but laugh. This is George every morning.

"Morning George," I say. He comes in and immediately looks for Lilly. My god do those two loves each other, best of friends, but sometimes they're like an old married couple.

"George shall we take your coat and shoes off sweetie?"

Sitting down, he begins to take his shoes off. I look to his mum when she starts to talk.

"He's had a rough night's sleep," she says. Bloody great, this is all I need on a Monday, a grumpy child. He'll be a nightmare today if he's tired. He will be falling asleep on my sofa this afternoon. "But please don't let him fall asleep later, he might sleep tonight then," she says. I want to roll my eyes at her, it's hard keeping a child awake, when all they want to do is sleep. Instead, smiling brightly I say, "Sure no problem."

After saying goodbye, we head into the playroom to the other two who are happily sat watching Paw Patrol, a kid's series, on TV.

I return to trying to make the playroom more like a room to play in. Once it's somewhat tidy I go into the kitchen to start the breakfast routine. Before long Jack and Ruby have arrived and all are fed and playing quietly. It's very rare this happens. Time soon passes and it's time for the school run.

"Right kids, time to tidy up and get ready."

Five minutes later we all bundle out the door, I must admit these kids are amazing at walking.

You have to love the school run. Always a bunch of clique mums who stand there, in their own little groups, no doubt bitching about other mums. I can't be arsed with them all, I don't need the drama. They're all fake and not who I want to be around. I walk over to Kelly, the other childminder who works this school, we haven't really known each other long, but she is so quiet. I feel like I need to bring her out her shell a bit. She is a lovely person and we could be good friends.

"Hey, Kelly, how's it going?" She looks across to me smiling.

"Yeah, all good thanks. Did you have a good weekend?" she asks.

"Yes thanks. Went way too quickly though. So, what's your plans for today?" I ask.

"Oh, nothing much. Staying at home with the kids."

How did I know she would say that? Kelly doesn't like to go out much, it seems she doesn't have much confidence in herself. When I've asked before, it's always the same answer.

"Do you fancy coming to soft play?" I ask.

She's silent while she thinks about it.

"Come on," I say. "The kids can play; we can chat and get to know each other."

"Yeah okay, go on then."

I'm mentally fist pumping the air. The teacher blows the whistle, and the kids go straight to line up. Grabbing George's hand, I begin pushing the pushchair towards the school gates.

"Shall we meet at ten am?" I say to Kelly

"Yeah, sounds good."

Saying goodbye, I walk home with the two kids I still have and think maybe this day might not be too bad after all.

Walking into the soft play a little while later, I notice it's quiet.

Thank god.

Finding a sofa, I put all my bags down and sort the kids out to go play. Five minutes later, Kelly arrives with her three kids. Smiling, I wave, and she comes over.

"Hi," I say to her. She smiles back and takes the kids coats off. "Do you want a drink?" She looks at the café then back to me.

"Yes please, Pepsi would be great." I go to the café and order our drinks. Going back to Kelly I see her sat watching the kids play.

"Here, love, your drink," I say as I pass it over to her.

"Thank you," she says.

We're sat while the kids play when I realise one of Kelly's children isn't in the toddler section.

"Oh crap," I mumble under a breath.

"What's up?"

"Tyler is missing."

The next minute we hear a high pitch scream coming from the bigger part of the soft play. Jumping up I rush to where the sound is coming from and see Tyler crying. Shouting for Kelly, she heads towards him along with another lady.

"What's wrong?" Kelly asks Tyler.

Tyler is screaming so loud he doesn't answer... seriously this kid could win the award for been the most over dramatic child. Rolling my eyes, I go to check the other kids are still okay.

Kelly comes over with a still screaming Tyler in her arms, along with another lady who also happens to be dragging a child along with her.

"I am so sorry," the lady says.

I look at her, puzzled. Tyler has calmed down at last, thank god, that child is so flipping loud. It turns out the other lady's child had bitten Tyler. He has a nice bite mark on his arm, you can see the teeth marks on him and it's already starting to bruise. That will be fun for Kelly explaining to his mum.

The other lady can't stop apologising.

"It's not a problem," Kelly says. "We all know what kids are like."

"My name's Georgia. I'm a childminder, so this little ratbag here isn't actually mine," she explains.

"Hey, me and Kelly here are childminders too, nice to meet you," I say to her.

"Nice to meet you too, I don't know any other childminders."

"It's a lonely job isn't it?" I say.

"Yes definitely, with only kids to talk to," Georgia says.

"Why don't you come join us? It would be nice to make more friends".

"Thank you, that would be fabulous."

The three of us spend the rest morning chatting away about anything and everything. We seem to just click with each other and I hope it will become a good friendship.

Chapter Two

Lucas

As I stand and stare at my son laying fast asleep in his cot, I think to myself that I did something right in this world. Looking all peaceful, I am reminded why I need to stay strong. I could have so easily been like my ex-wife. Just walked away, without a backwards glance, but as I stand and look at him, I wonder how anyone can walk away from him. I love him with my whole body, there's nothing I wouldn't do for him. He is my world. He is beyond a doubt the most gorgeous little boy. I might be bias, but he is. I walk out his room, head downstairs and flop on the sofa.

Ben and I walked away from my soon to be ex-wife about two months ago. He is only a couple of weeks away from his first birthday and I have everything planned for him. Not that he will know what the hell is going on, but for my sake, I need to do this for him. My family are coming around with my brother's kids for a small get together. I have the cake and presents all good to go. If only the rest of my life was as organised.

Deciding I need to do something, I pull the laptop open and have a look at a website my brother mentioned about childcare. Opening the browser and typing the web address, the Perfect Childcare website appears on the screen. After talking to several people, I decided a childminder would be the better option. They have more freedom to go out and he will mix with different ages in a homely atmosphere. Also, having just one person caring for him will be more stable. He's already being passed around so much. So, having just one person looking after him would be better. I'm not keen on nurseries and how they operate. Pulling up the list of childminders I start looking through some profiles, but soon enough my eyes become heavy, I give up. Making my way to bed I flop down, being a single dad is hard work. I need some help and the sooner the better.

Waking the next morning to my little boy chatting away on the baby monitor, is something I could listen to all day. I make my way to his room and his little face lights up when he sees me, it warms my heart. He really does make my days' worth while. Heading downstairs, I sit him in his high chair and turn on the coffee machine. No day can begin without my daily fix of caffeine. While waiting for the coffee to brew, I begin making his breakfast.

"So little man what shall we do today?" I ask. I have the week off to help take off the pressure off my family. His response is his sweet little laugh. "You want to do that do you?" I say with a smile. I love our one-sided conversations.

After breakfast we make our way to the living room, I place Ben down to play. Noticing my laptop sitting there from where I left it last night, I open it up. I may as well have another nosey at childminders. Bringing up the profiles again I begin searching, narrowing the search down to within a two miles radius. I don't want to have to drive all over the city. It will be close to work as well, in case of emergencies.

I continue scrawling until I come across a profile that's only a few minutes away, feeling drawn to it I click to find out more. I'm left breathless at the profile picture starring back at me. Fuck me, she's gorgeous. I'm sitting there staring, like a horny teenager with their first playboy magazine. She has the most stunning ocean blue eyes I've ever seen. I force my gaze away and look at her profile. Everything about her seems perfect. she has all the qualifications my brother said to look for. She has her first aid, that's important to me. She also has her level three in home-based childcare, that's good. Deciding to take a chance, I send a message.

Closing the laptop, I potter about the house doing various jobs until lunch. After lunch I decide to go for a walk with Ben, get us some fresh air. I feel better now I've made a start on looking for childcare for him, I have a little spring in my step knowing I'm doing what's best for him. Once ready, I sit him in his pushchair, make my way out the door and head towards the play park, that's not that far from here. Ben loves the swings.

As we approach the park, I look to see a young lady sat on the bench with a couple of kids already playing on the slide. Staring for longer than appropriate, I can't help but feel like I've seen her before. Realising it's the childminder I messaged this morning; I stand back and watch her interaction with the kids. The children seem to adore her. When one falls over and starts to cry, straight away she is by her side comforting her. I watch in awe at how lovely she is with them. Tearing my gaze away I decide to leave the park. Seeing her today, I pray she can help me with Ben. Only time will tell.

By the time we get home, Ben's fallen asleep in his pushchair. Leaving him in the hallway, I head into the living room, I sit down on the sofa and take advantage of having five minutes quiet. My peace is disturbed by a knocking at the door, which wakes up Ben and he starts screaming.

"For fuck's sake" I grumble before getting up and going to see who it is. Opening the door, I find my brother, Mike, with his son, Daniel.

"What do you want?" I ask, before seeing to Ben, who is still screaming in the pushchair.

"You're in a good mood."

I turn and glare at him while picking Ben up.

"What do you expect, you woke him up." I snap,

"How the fuck did I know he was asleep?" he states.

"Watch your mouth Mike," I bark. Walking in to the living room to sit down with a still sleepy Ben. Mike follows and places Daniel on the floor. He's is just coming up for two year's old and is a complete hurricane. You can bet your arse everything will be trashed soon. I swear this kid is on some sort of amphetamine.

"So why you here?" I ask him.

"Julie and I were thinking, me and you need a night out. Julie's happy to have Ben and we can go grab a few drinks. What do you think?

"Yes," I shout, making Ben jump a mile out my arms. "Whoops, sorry baby boy" I soothe, chuckling to myself.

Placing Ben on the floor after he calms down, I look to Mike.

"Yes. You have no idea how much I need that."

A genuine smile appears on his face. After sorting a date to go out, Mike and Daniel leave. I smile, as I'm feeling good for the first time in ages.

Chapter Three

Charlie

Looking down at my phone when I hear it beep, I notice I have a message on the childcare website I am registered on. Clicking open the message I see the face of a gorgeous curly-haired little boy in the profile picture. Glancing down to the message I begin reading.

> Dear Charlie.
>
> I'm looking for reliable childcare for my nearly one-year old son, Ben. I require care for him Monday to Friday 7.30-4.30. This little boy means everything to me and I just want what's best for him. If you can help in anyway, please do message me back.
>
> Kind regards, Lucas.

After reading the message over and over, I feel something inside, I could feel the desperation his message. Something was calling me to help this man and his son. I know I have the space available and can help, so it's a no brainier for me. Making sure the kids are happy playing in the park, I begin typing my message back to him.

Dear Lucas.

Thank you for the message, I do have space in my setting to be able have your little boy. If you would like to come and visit my home and meet me, we can then talk more about your requirements.

Regards Charlie.

Putting my phone back in my pocket I call all the kids over for a drink and a snack. After playing a little more, I decide that its best to make our way back home. Walking along my phone beeps again in my pocket. Thinking it's a message back about the little boy I'm surprised to see a text from Kelly. Deciding I will read it when back, I place my phone back in my pocket. Arriving home, the kids all run into the living room to play. Seeing i's nearly dinnertime, I put my bag away and begin preparing food for dinner. When the kids are settled eating. I reach for my phone and read Kelly's message.

Kelly: Hey bitch, we need a night out, can you get a babysitter for Holly?

Me: Hey tit face, let me see what I can do, when you thinking?

Kelly: How about 22nd?

Me: Yeah sounds good. Leave it with me and will let you know. Is Georgia coming out as well?

Kelly: I will message and ask her now. Speak soon, bitch.

Chuckling to myself I bring up Mum's number and press call. She answers straight away, like she always does.

"Hey mum, any chance you can have Holly for me overnight on the twenty-second?"

"Yeah sure I can, you know I will always have my granddaughter anytime."

"Thanks, mum you're a star," I happily say. We chat some more before saying goodbye.

Me: Hey all sorted, mum is having her overnight... woohoo.

Kelly: Yay. Georgia is down for it as well! Drinks are happening.

Me: Can't freaking wait. Speak soon tit face.

After finishing up with dinner and doing a nappy change, I begin getting sorted for the kids going home.

When all the children are collected at the end of my working day, I decide a nice quiet evening is in order. I've got a small headache coming on and just want to relax. After getting dinner out of the way, for myself and Holly, I take her into the living room. After a quick tidy up, my phone beeps in my pocket making me groan.

"What now?" I mutter. Pulling my phone out I see I have reply about that little boy.

Dear Charlie.
Thank you so much for responding, meeting you would be great. I'm free all week so whatever is an easy time and day for you.
Lucas

Thinking about my week, I reply straight away.

Dear Lucas
Is Wednesday around one-thirty pm okay with you?
Charlie

Putting my phone back in my pocket I look to Holly sat watching TV.

"Hey baby, shall we go have your bath and get ready for bed?"

She responds with a big yawn, and we make our way upstairs to begin her nightly, bedtime routine.

Once Holly is settled in bed, I pour myself a glass of wine. Taking the first sip, I sigh in contentment. Bliss. My phone buzzes in my pocket again, I pull it out to read the message confirming the meeting. Replying with my address I walk into the living room and place my phone on the arm of the sofa. Flicking through the channels on the TV, I settle on watching the Simpsons.

My mind drifts to the curly-haired little boy I am meeting in a couple of days. I can't put my finger on it, but something is pulling me to that boy. He is utterly gorgeous with such big chocolaty brown eyes. I shake my thoughts away, and start yawning away, so I decide to call it a night.

The next day I meet up with the girls at the local music bounce group. Holly absolutely loves this group; she loves the puppets and I swear to god she can sing nearly all the songs. We have the CD in the car, and I swear to god, one of these days an accident is going to happen to it, if I must fucking listen to it anymore.

"Oh, I have a meeting tomorrow for a nearly one-year old little boy. There is something about this little boy that I can't put my finger on."

Kelly looks at me puzzled.

"What do you mean?" she asks.

"I don't know, it's hard to explain, but looking at his picture, I just felt this pull to him. Guess we'll see what tomorrow brings" I say, both girls just look at me, unsure what to say.

I just have this gut feeling that this meeting tomorrow is going be anything like my normal meetings for children. As I say, only time will tell.

After the group is finished, I say goodbye to the girls and head home. Both kids are exhausted and fall asleep literally just before we get home.

"For fuck sake" I grumble under my breath. "Why? Why do they fall asleep just before we get home?" I moan to no-one. Looks like I am sitting in the car a while now. Good job I have my kindle app on my phone, time to lose myself in my latest book boyfriend.

Today's my day off. I don't have children contracted on Wednesdays during school hours. Hopefully this meeting today will change that. Holly is happily playing with her toys, so I potter about making sure the house is clean. I also make sure to have all my files put on the table for this meeting. It's amazing what is needed. I have fifteen policies including safe guarding, collection, behaviour just to name a few. Qualification certificates, all other paperwork for the parent to fill in. This is one of the downsides to the job. Well that and fucking Ofsted.

After lunch I put Holly in bed and make sure everything is in place. Suddenly the doorbell goes, walking over to the door I open it and gasp. Holy fucking hell… the man stood before me is the most gorgeous man I have ever laid eyes on. Jesus Christ, I roam my eyes down the length of him, he is fine. He looks like he has toned body from either his job or going to the gym. He is easily six-foot tall and dressed in casual clothes of jeans and a black fitted t-shirt. Man does it hug his body like a glove. Looking up I stare in to his eyes…. I am fucked.

Chapter Four

Lucas

Fuck me. I'm standing starring in to the most gorgeous ocean, blue eyes I've ever seen. I knew she was gorgeous, but now standing here I am completely knocked off my feet at how gorgeous she really is. I run my eyes down the length of her and something in me itches to reach over and pull her into my arms. Shaking away my thoughts, I look up to her eyes again. We stand looking at each before I clear my throat.

"Hi, I am Lucas."

Giving me a small smile, she composes herself.

"Hi, yes hello, I'm Charlie, please do come in."

I chuckle to myself at her been slightly flustered. Picking up the changing bag I had placed on the step next to me, I make my way inside. I walk into a gorgeous fitted kitchen, made up off duck egg coloured units and white walls. It's decorated nicely and feels so homely.

"Please walk through," she says, pointing to the other room. I walk through to the living room, and straight away know I would be more than happy leaving Ben here. As I look around, I notice all the toys neatly in boxes in a tall Ikea unit. There is also a toy kitchen to one side and a small table with some stools under it.

"Please sit down," she says, pointing to the sofa. I make myself comfy with Ben on my lap. Charlie walks over to a toy box in the unit, begins selecting some toys and brings them over.

"Hello gorgeous boy, you have the most gorgeous brown eyes I have ever seen," Charlie says to Ben as she hands him a toy, which he grabs straight away and puts straight in his mouth.

"Sorry, everything goes in his mouth now"

"Please don't worry" she says. "Everything gets cleaned weekly," she informs me.

Straight away I feel at ease in her company. I don't know what it is, but there is something about her.

"So, tell me more about this little fellow and what childcare requirements you need," Charlie says breaking me away from my thoughts.

"This is Ben. He's just coming up one-years-old in about a week or so time."

"You said in your message you would need seven-thirty to four-thirty, is that still correct?" she asks me,

"Yes, if that's possible, it would be Monday to Friday."

"That's fine, would you require me to provide food?" she asks.

I look at her and suddenly feel a bit overwhelmed by it all. She notices the sudden change in me and must notice the look on my face, because she moves to come sit next to me.

"Hey, it's okay, if it's too much we can take a break, would you like a drink?" She asks me, I smile at her gesture and give her a nod.

"Yes please, water would be great, thank you."

Charlie walks into the kitchen and I place Ben down on the floor with the toys Charlie got out for him. Charlie walks back into the room with two bottles of waters.

"Hope bottled is okay?" She asks, "I find it easier with the kids with having a lid on," she says chuckling.

"Yes, that's perfect, thank you," I say smiling at her.

Sitting back down she hands me the water. Taking a small swig of it, I feel myself relax a little. Looking over I smile when I catch Charlie watching me. Knowing she has been caught, a small, pink blush covers her cheeks.

"Sorry about earlier, it's just so hard. I'm a single dad and this little man is my absolute world. I just find it all so confusing thinking what childcare I need. I am completely clueless to it all." Smiling a big smile, I find that she really does put me at ease

"Why don't I make it easier for you and explain what I do," she says.

Thirty minutes later, she has explained everything and showed me all her paperwork. Which at first just baffled me completely, but with her explanations I slowly started to understand it all. She really does seem to know her stuff and watching her briefly with Ben, she genuinely seems to like looking after children. Ben has taken to her straight away, which has made this decision so much easier.

"Do you mind me asking about his mum? It's just I like to know everything to make it easier if things come up later." Charlie looks a little unsure at first as I fidget in my seat. Talking about this is never easy.

"His mum is not around. She walked away from him about two months ago. I have pretty much raised him myself since the day he was born," I tell her.

"I am so sorry, I don't know how anyone could walk away from him, he is utterly gorgeous," she replies. There is a genuine look of anger on her face when she says this.

"It's, okay" I say to her. "I've accepted who she is, but at the moment it will be me who will always be around for Ben. My ex-wife isn't to come here. She won't even know about you," I explain to her.

"That's fine, I only release children from my care to those I know. If I ever meet your ex-wife, I wouldn't ever let her take him, especially without you telling me do so," she informs me.

This puts me at ease a little more.

"Thank you for today, I feel completely happy with everything you have said and would absolutely love for you to look after Ben. He seems happy and that's my main priority really."

She smiles at me and genuinely looks pleased.

"Thank you that's great to hear. I would love to have this little monster."

I chuckle at her comment, Ben can be a little monster at times, but I wouldn't have him any other way.

After exchanging numbers and getting all the paperwork sorted, I get set to leave. Walking towards the door, I hold my hand out and she places her hand in mine, tingles like nothing I've felt before, shoot right up my arm. She must feel it too because suddenly she pulls her hand away. Looking all flustered she stutters her words, "Err nice to meet you and I... I will b... be in touch about settling Ben in."

Quickly thanking her I make my way out the door. I have no idea what that was. My brain can't make head or tails of it.

Making my way to the car, I strap Ben in his seat and make my way round to the driver's side and climb in. Sitting there for a few minutes, my mind wonders to the woman I have just met and her stunning blue eyes. I know Ben is going to be in capable, caring hands, and that's makes me feel better, but I just feel my heart beats faster when I think of her. I need to get a grip on myself, I don't need anything to come of this. I especially don't want to risk her not being able to look after my son. With that thought in mind, I start the car and make my way home.

The next day, I drop Ben to my mums and make my way to work. I have my own company building furniture with my brother. We have built up a good reputation now, word has got around about us and we are doing pretty good. Don't get me wrong I can't retire yet, but I am earning enough to be comfortable. Making my way inside I head to the back of the workshop to where Mike is.

"Hey" I say. Mike looks up to me.

"Thought you had this week off?" he asks me.

"Yeah, but I thought I would come in and help today. Mum wanted to see Ben, so I would have only been left twiddling my thumbs," I explain.

"How did the childcare meeting go yesterday?" he asks while looking around for what, I don't know.

"Yeah it was good. Ben is going to start there in two weeks," I say, while refusing to meet my brother's eyes.

"What you not telling me?" He looks at me with raised brows… "Is this childminder hot or something?"

I gasp at what he has just said and look down to the floor.

"She is, isn't she?" he says with a shit eating grin on his face. "Oh. My. God. This is hilarious," he says while laughing his head off.

"Piss off will you. She was lovely and very professional. Yes, she maybe beautiful, but you know I'm not bothering with anyone right now. I need to be there for Ben and I don't need any more drama in my life.

"Look man, don't let what happened with Molly put you off, you of all people deserve to be happy. Ben is a happy little thing and that's all your doing. Just don't rule out any sort of future," he says with sympathy in his eyes.

I know what he is saying is true, but I just don't think I am ready for anything right now, but then why does my thoughts keep going back to Charlie. There is just something about her that I just can't quite put my finger on. Shaking my thoughts away, I ask my brother what needs doing and get to work.

That evening while having a cuddle with Ben my thoughts drift back to the day me and Molly found out she was pregnant...

Walking through the door after work I know straight away something is not right. I enter the living room and I'm confronted with a very hard face Molly.

"What's going on"? I ask.

She turns to face me with such a scowl on her face. My heart rate picks up and I find myself starting to worry. She is scaring me... My mind is running a million miles a minute, coming up with all sorts of things that could have happened.

Has someone died?

Is she hurt?

Although doing a quick glance over her she seems okay, there is nothing showing to explain what is going on.

Walking over to her I squat down in front of her and hold her hands.

"Sweetheart, your scaring me. What's wrong"? I ask her again.

Her eyes meet mine; they look so dark and it's like all life has vanished from them...

"I'm pregnant" she says...

Everything around me stops. My brain suddenly catches up with what she has just said...

She's pregnant.

This is amazing news.

So why does she look like she has a face like thunder and her whole world has ended?

I suddenly jump up. "That's fantastic" I say..." Oh. My. God. I'm going to be a dad." I look to Molly again and she is just sat there, not saying a word. "Aren't you happy?" I ask her

"Happy. You want me to be happy? This is the worst fucking news ever," she shouts at me.

I stand there with my mouth open in shock. I know we never really discussed children before now, but I honestly thought it was in our future.

She starts pacing the room, you can physically see the steam coming from her.

"I don't understand, I always thought you liked children?"

"Yes, I do, but that doesn't mean I fucking want them." she states angrily.

I'm completely at a loss as to want to say. Suddenly a horrible feeling comes over me. Walking up to her I ask her something I really don't want to know the answer to.

"You're not thinking of getting rid of this baby, are you?"

She's looking at me, and I see no emotion whatsoever in her eyes. It's like her mind is already made up and my heart is breaking. I never in my life saw this coming. I know she loves her life with her friends, but I've seen her with her sister's kids and she loves them. I don't understand any of this.

"Now that would be the best fucking solution ever, but you and I both know my family would disown me if they ever found out," she states with such hatred. "Nope, it looks like I

am stuck with this baby now, but I am telling you, you're the one getting up in the fucking night with IT," she tells me, before storming out the room.

I drop down on the sofa... my mind is just in a complete mess. No, it will be fine I think to myself. She will bond with baby while pregnant and you'll see. She will fall in love with he or she when peanut is born. I just hope to god I am right...

For the first time since hearing the news I let the biggest smile cover my face.

I am going to be a dad.

I cannot wait...

He or she will have so much love.

With that thought I pull my phone out my pocket, call my brother and tell him the news.

Looking back now, I now know how wrong I was. Molly hated Ben from the minute he was born. She was so worried about what her family would think if she terminated the pregnancy, but where are they all now? Not one of them has seen Ben in nearly two months. Even when me and Molly where together they didn't come around much to see him. If it wasn't for my family, I would have crumbled.

No, getting out of my marriage was the best decision for me and Ben. He has enough love from my family. He doesn't need any more and now he will have a lovely childminder who will care for him like her own. I just know it. She was so caring and understanding with me. Ben is going to be so happy there...

I just need to keep my own feelings hidden away.

Chapter Five

Charlie

Closing the door after saying goodbye to Lucas, I stare at the it and try and wrap my head around what just happened. Never in my life have I felt such tingles, like when I touched his hand. I can still feel the sensation now. Making my way back to the living room, I plonk my arse down and just sit there. I know without a doubt Holly is going to be awake very soon, she only has about an hour's sleep. Also, we must go get the kids from school in about twenty minutes.

My mind drifts to Lucas, he is unbelievably sexy. When he was taking a swig of his water, I just couldn't help but stare at his arms. He obviously works out, I'm not sure when he finds the time. Unless it's his job. Picking up the paperwork he filled in I notice that he's written that he is a carpenter by trade. Hmm, he may come in handy when I need some things built for the garden. I've been thinking for a while now I need a new climbing frame for the older kids. Noticing the time, I make my way upstairs and wake Holly up.

"Hey baby girl," I say to her. Picking her up from the bed, she's still sleepy and lays her head on my shoulder.

"I take it your still tired," I say chuckling. Making my way downstairs I get the pushchair out, strapping her in, I set off for school to collect the kids. I am collecting four today so it will be an easy afternoon.

By the time the last child has left for the day, even with only working before and after school. I am shattered. I set about tidying the Lego away from the little table and all the fucking Hama beads from the big table, the kids love making things with these. They place little beads on boards to make up pictures, only issue is, I have to iron them to set them together. I fucking hate these things; you can bet your arse I will still be finding them on the floor for the next few days. Once the room is tidy, I make my way upstairs to run bath and put Holly to bed. Placing her in her room to play, I go to the bathroom. Pulling my phone from my pocket I decide to text Kelly.

Me: Hey tit face, I know its Wednesday and a school night, but you fancy coming around for a drink?

Turning the tap off in the bath, I go and grab Holly. After washing her and getting her ready for bed, we have our usual bedtime story, which she always falls asleep to. Switching on her night light, I make my way downstairs. My phone buzzes, so pull it out and to check the message.

Kelly: Hell Yeah. Will be round in two, bringing Georgia. She is pissed off.

Me: Oh, dear what's he done now?

Kelly: LOL. You know it all so well. She will explain all. On our way.

Me: See you soon tit face.

Walking into the kitchen I grab the wine and some glasses. By sounds of it, we are going to need it. Two minutes later the girls come walking in.

"Hey bitches," I greet them both. Kelly comes walking in followed by a rather glum looking Georgia.

"What's up girl," I say to Georgia. "Edward being a dick again?"

Georgia throws her head back and full on belly laughs.

"Damn girl you really do know how to make me laugh."

Just like that the gloomy mood lifts. We spend the evening putting the world to rights. Georgia informs me what's gone on with her dick of a husband. I fill them in on my meeting, leaving out the part of when our hands touch. I don't know what to make of it, never mind them two.

After two bottles of wine, the girls make their way home. I set about cleaning up and making sure everything is set for morning. Once done, I make my way up to bed. Crawling in, I sigh with relief when my head hits the pillow. Picking up my kindle I decide to read a couple of chapters of my latest book. Whilst I was getting lost in my book, I find myself drifting off to sleep.

Suddenly I find I'm shooting my eyes open when my kindle hits in my face. Yep time for sleep I think… switching it off and placing it on my bedside cabinet, I turn over and fall into a blissful sleep, with dreams filled of a dark-haired man, with a gorgeous smile.

The next morning, I'm awoken by my alarm blaring, and feel like I've not had any sleep. Switching off the alarm, I roll over and stretch my body. I am seriously in need of a holiday.

"Shit that reminds me, I must message Lucas my holidays for the year." We didn't discuss that yesterday. Right best get my arse up for another fun-filled working day, I think sarcastically.

Later that day me and girls are walking round the farm looking at all the animals. We decided on going yesterday, I know George who I care for, loves animals. Georgia and Kelly both have two children each, who love it as well. Longdown Dairy Farm is amazing and lets the children become hands on with the animals.

"Are we still going out next week?" I ask them both.

I get a 'Hell yeah,' from them both, which makes me chuckle, while I make my way to the small animal petting area. Sitting George down on the bales of hay, I place a small chick in his hands. I would hand Holly one, but she just squeezes them to death. Seeing the children smiling and having fun, makes this day a success.

"Smile George," I say to him, trying to get a photo to send to his mum. In response I get a seriously weird grin. I can't help but burst out laughing, his mum is going to love this pic. As it nears lunch time, we make our way over to the picnic area. Sitting the kids down on a picnic bench, I suddenly remember I need to text Lucas about my holiday dates. Pulling out my phone I search for his name.

Me: Hi Lucas, its Charlie. I thought I would let you know my holidays for the rest of this year. I have two weeks booked in August from the tenth, and then have two weeks off at Christmas. I finish on the twenty-second. If you require any childcare for while I'm unavailable, then please let me know. Have a good day.

Placing my phone back in my bag, I sit and eat my lunch with the girls and kids. Today has been a good day and the kids have been so well behaved. It's a day like this that I really do enjoy my job. Making my way back to the car, I make it home in time to collect Lilly from school. Once I get back home from school with the kids, I notice I have a message on my phone. Pulling up the message app, I notice it's from Lucas.

Lucas: Hi Charlie. Thank you for these dates, but don't worry if you ever need any more time off it's not a problem

for me. I can have family help me out or just have the day off myself. Hope having a good day. It's hot outside, please don't overdo it. Lucas

Re-reading the message I think to myself… wow, I wish all my parents were like him about needing time off. Fuck me sideways, I will keep him. Looking at the message again I look at the emoji he has used, it makes me smile. Why is he being so thoughtful? I'm pulled from my thoughts when shouting comes from the living room, looks like Lilly and George are up to no good again. They're like an old married couple them two. Walking in the room I say to them, "What's going on in here."

Both kids jump because they weren't aware, I was in the room with them, both are looking sheepish, it's then I notice Lilly has something behind her back.

"Lilly what are you hiding?" I ask.

"Nothing Charlie," she states with a grin on her face…

Hmm, I wonder, I walk over to where she is and try to see what she has.

"Let me see now please," I ask in my firm voice. Pulling George's toy dinosaur from behind her back I groan…

How the hell did he get that out his box without me seeing. I swear to god; I am banning all toys from home coming to my house. Looking at George, I tell him, "I will deal with you in a minute, okay George."

"Now you, young lady know better than taking toys off other children, what do you say?" I ask her

"Sorry," she says, while looking down with tears forming in her eyes…

"Now George why have you got this? You know not to take it from your box." I ask him…

George just stands there and refuses to answer me. Why do I do this job again…? Holly bless her heart is just sat there playing beautifully with the mega blocks.

"Right both of you play nicely together, I will be doing dinner soon, before it's home time." Walking away I place his dinosaur back in his box. I really must remind parents, yet again that there are to be no toys to brought from home.

It's Friday today so I've decided to have a quiet day in with Holly and George after the other kids have gone to school. I'm sat playing with some puzzles with Holly, when the doorbell goes.

"Stay there kids," I tell them as I make my way to the door. Opening the it, I am greeted with a well-dressed lady in a blue skirt and jacket, paired with a lovely pink, silk blouse.

"Charlie James?" she asks me… "I am Jennifer Brooke, I'm here from Ofsted." She says showing me her badge that's around her neck.

Oh fuck…. The expression on my face must show that I'm shocked.

"May I come in please, and please don't worry." she says.

"Yes, sorry come in." I move to the side and allow her to come in to my home. Fuck I wasn't expecting a visit at all. My brain starts going in to panic mode now and my hands start sweating...

Shit, Shit, Shit.

Why is she here? My brain is going into overdrive.

"Would you like a drink?" I ask her.

"Yes, water would be lovely please," she says while walking into the living room. While I go about getting her a bottle of water, I quickly fire of a group text to the girls.

Me: Fuck, Fuck, Fuck, Fuck. Ofsted have just turned up... What the hell. Be back later when she has gone.

Placing my phone on the side, I make my way into the living room and hand her the water. Sitting down I start wringing my hands together in nervousness. I honestly have no idea why she is here. I'm good at my job and normally for a routine inspection you get a least a couple days' notice. Unannounced visits usually mean a complaint. I feel like I'm on the verge of tears, my hands are sweating, and I can't stop shaking. Jennifer notices my composure and tries to reassure me.

"Please relax Charlie, I am not here to strike you off, we've received a complaint about a child in your care," she explains.

That's it, my heart stops, I can't breathe and I feel like I am drowning. Who would complain about me?

"From the look on your face I can see this is completely new to you?" She asks me.

"Yes, I honestly have no idea what I could have done wrong." I'm racking my brain trying to find a slight clue as to what it could be about, but I am coming up with nothing, nothing at all.

"Sorry I'm so confused by this, my families are happy with my care, no-one has left lately. Nothing has happened out of the ordinary." I tell her.

"The complaint is about a little boy who supposedly walked away from you at school and walked out the main school gates," she informs me.

What the fuck. I think I know exactly what she is on about and it fucking didn't happen like that. I swear to god, I find out who said this, they better run a fucking mile.

"Yes, I know what you're talking about and can tell you now it wasn't anything like that."

I begin to tell her all about George walking out of the year one gate and standing outside. He was only about a foot away from me. Kelly had come over and brought him back through the gate and joked about me losing someone. He didn't walk out the fucking main gates. I am so angry, it's unreal. We go through everything, showing her all my paperwork and she leaves happy with what I've explained. No further action is needed. Thank god. I have a grade rating of Good now and would hate to lose it. After she leaves, I message the girls again.

Me: All over. I am so fucking angry girls. Some bastard has complained about me.

Kelly: Oh my God. What the fuck? What about?

Me: Remember when George walked out of the year one gates and you got him? Some fucker has said he walked out the main gates, away from me.

Kelly: Absolute fucker.

Georgia: Sorry girl's explosive nappy, what have I missed?

Me: Some twat complaining about me to Ofsted. I need a fucking drink.

Georgia: You're fucking joking me?

Kelly: Wish she was. How was it left?

Me: Yeah, all good. She was happy when I explained what happened, so that's good. Any way girls, I need to sort lunch out for these two munchkins. Will message you both later.

Kelly: Bye lovely, we think you're amazing.

Smiling at that last message I place my phone on the side and begin making lunch for the kids. I need a bottle of wine tonight, thank fuck it's Friday. Walking to the fridge I notice I have no wine. I groan under my breath, I guess I am off to the shop after work now. The rest of the day passes quickly, which is a bloody good job really.

When all the children have left for the day, I get myself and Holly ready for the trip to the shop for my much needed wine. Locking the house up, I make my way over to the car with Holly. After strapping Holly in her seat, I walk around to the driver's side, climb in and drive to the nearest supermarket. Walking down the aisles I come to the section I need. Dropping Hollys hand, I stand staring at the all the bottles in front of me. After staring for a about a minute or two, I select the same bottle I always go for. Turning to grab Hollys hand again, I notice she's gone.

"Holly," I shout and start frantically searching all the aisles for her. My heart is beating so hard, it feels like it's going to burst free from my chest. Where is she? Suddenly I hear her sweet voice. Turning around I come face to face with Lucas with Ben in his arms and Holly by his side.

"Take it she belongs to you?" he says.

"Oh. My. God, Holly, you gave me a heart attack, don't ever walk away from me again," I say picking her up and squeezing her hard.

"Thank you so much, after today you have no idea how much more trouble, I would be in." I explain. He looks at me in confusion. I tell him about the events of today, I might as well, as I am planning on informing all my parents about it. I don't hide anything from any of them and he is going to be one of them in about weeks' time. While telling him I can feel the tears start to prick my eyes. Today has been one major cluster fuck, I just want to curl up in bed and forget about it all. Lucas notices my tears, lifts his hand, and wipes a lone tear that falls away. My breath catches in my throat at the contact.

"Please don't cry," he says looking at me with such soft eyes. I try my hardest not to cry some more, I need to leave. I can't be here with a parent acting the way I am.

"Sorry, you must think I am totally nut's. Not the best impression for your new childminder. Thank you for finding Holly. I can't thank you enough."

With that said I quickly turn on my heels and walk away. Making my way to the checkout I pay for my wine and get the hell home. I can't believe I've just cried in front of one of my new parents. Who does that?

After getting home, I get Holly ready for bed and quickly read her a bedtime story. Once she's asleep I make my way back downstairs. Walking into my living room, I collapse on the sofa and pour myself a big glass of wine. I honestly just want this day to be over with. Suddenly I hear my phone beeping. Realising I left it in the kitchen, I groan at being disturbed and debate on whether to ignoring it or not. Damn it's probably important, getting up, I go and see who it is. Picking my phone up I notice it's a message from Lucas and my heart rate picks up. What the hell is wrong with me? I open the message to read it.

Lucas: Sorry to message you, I just wanted to check you're okay?

I stand and stare at my phone… I don't know how to respond. I want to reply to him, but would it be classed as unprofessional? I walk back in the living room with my phone still in my hand. I decide a short little message back will be okay. I mean, I don't want to ignore him at all. With my mind made up I message him back.

Me: Thank you for asking, I 'm much better now.

There short and sweet. Placing my phone next me I pick up my wine and carry on watching the series Friends. You can never tire of watching this program. When my phone beeps again I look at it in shock, surely, he hasn't message me back? Lifting my phone up I glance down at the message on the screen.

Lucas: I am so pleased, you had me a little worried there. If you ever want to talk, I am always around.

Wow, just wow... I'm lost for words; I've never had a parent interested like this before. I have always stayed professional, kept my personal life and work life separate. Reading his message again, my heart skips a beat. I have no idea what it is about this guy, but he has me feeling all sorts of things I know I really shouldn't be feeling. Deciding to not message back, I finish my wine and decide to go to bed. Thank god it's the weekend.

Chapter Six

Lucas

I have just watched Charlie rush away from me and I have

to fight everything in me not to go after her. When I saw how upset she was, all I wanted to do was pull her to me. To hold her and protect her from the world. I have never felt anything like it before, not even with Molly. She makes me feel like me again. Like I can be happy again.

Walking back to my car, I get Ben strapped in his seat, and get in the driver's side, and make my way home so I can get Ben ready for bed. He is starting to get grumpy and wanting his bottle.

Arriving home, I get Ben settled in bed, then make my way downstairs, take a seat on the sofa and switch on the TV. I can't seem to concentrate on watching anything, Charlie is plaguing my thoughts. I can't seem to get that gorgeous woman out of my head. Needing to know she is okay; I grab my phone and shoot a message off to her asking if she is okay. I know I should stay well clear, it's not like we are friends. She is going to be my son's childminder for Christ sake. Our relationship should remain professional, but there is just something about this woman that has me doing weird stuff. She's caring, and I see the way she is with the children, I love that quality about her.

My phone suddenly buzzes letting me know I have a message back from her. Glancing down I read it. It's short and sweet, making me think she doesn't want to talk… I should just leave it at that, but I know that I won't. I've lost my mind.

Thinking about what she told me today, my blood starts to boil. I may have only seen her a couple of times and I don't really know her that well, but I can tell she is the sweetest and most caring person ever. If I didn't think that, she wouldn't be having Ben. I don't hear anything back after the last message I sent. I've probably scared her, and she thinks I am a right weirdo, I think laughing to myself. I decide to call it a night, today has knackered me out so I head to bed.

Looking in on Ben quickly, I notice he has kicked his covers off. Tucking him in, I make my way to my room, and go through my nightly routine before getting in to bed. My sleep is filled with dreams of a blonde haired, beauty, with stunning ocean blue eyes.

The next week flies by and by Thursday I'm shattered.

Ben is off for a small session tomorrow with Charlie, to see how he gets on. I'm so nervous it's unreal. I know he'll be fine and is in good hands, but still doesn't make worry any less. It the first time that he is being left with someone that's not family.

I get everything sorted that night, making sure he has enough nappies, wipes, and spare clothes. He'll probably won't need them, but for my own sanity I pack them anyway. I'm hoping from next week things will become easier for me and I can get myself in to somewhat of a normal routine. From Monday he starts with Charlie full-time. I just hope tomorrow goes okay and I'm not left having to change my plans.

'D' day arrives and before I know it, I'm heading over to

Charlie's. The closer I get, the more my heart rate picks up. I don't know if it's the thought of leaving Ben there for the first time, or it's the fact that I'll be seeing her.

Arriving at her house, I park my car and get Ben out. Walking down the path towards her door, I take in her garden. Charlie has it set up with some amazing toys. I do notice she doesn't have a climbing frame; I will have to ask her if it is something, she ever thought of having. Maybe it's something I can build for her over time. I push that thought to the back of my head and ring the doorbell. Charlie answers the door looking gorgeous as ever. She is wearing some tight, figure-hugging jeans that mould to her figure perfectly, she has it paired with a sexy, red floaty top. Seriously what is wrong with me, I shouldn't be having these thoughts about her.

"Hey Lucas, hey gorgeous boy." I hear her say, bringing me out my thoughts. Shaking my head, I look to Charlie and see she has a slight smirk on her face. She bloody knows what I was thinking I swear. Handing over Ben, I place his bag on his peg. It's so cute that he has his own little picture and name above the peg. Looking at Ben, I say goodbye and make sure all is good and walk away. Ben's not even taking any notice of me leaving.

I have two hours to kill now while he is there. Needing to keep myself busy, I head on over to work to see how it's all going there. I also need to check with my brother that we're still on for tonight. I am in desperate need of this night out.

Arriving at work I notice Mike's wife, Julie is there, she must be dropping lunch off for him. She does this often when he forgets it. Walking into the workshop I find my brother has Julie pinned to the wall kissing the hell out of her.

"Come on guys I don't need to see that," I state. Both jump apart in shock, serves themselves right, I think laughing.

"Jesus Christ Lucas you scared the shit out of us," my brother says.

I stand there laughing hard, I just can't help myself. Julie walks over to me and kisses me on the cheek.

"Hey, you, where's my gorgeous boy?" She asks.

"I've dropped him off at the childminder for a settling in session, he's there for two hours," I explain to her. "We still on for tonight?"

"Yep, I can't wait to spend some time with my gorgeous nephew, oh and make sure you bring his night time stuff for me."

I smile at how she likes to order me around; she knows it always works. She has me wrapped around her finger. Julie makes my brother happy and that's what I like. After chatting some more and agreeing a time to take Ben round, I make my way back to Charlie's.

Arriving at Charlie's I press the doorbell and wait patiently for her to answer. After a waiting a minute or so I start to wonder where she is. Pressing the doorbell again I hear noise coming from inside, then suddenly the door flies open.

"Sorry, I was changing Holly's nappy," she explains.

Nodding, she allows me inside. I walk through the kitchen to the living room, where Ben is currently sat in a big bouncy, funny looking contraption. Charlie must notice my confusion as to what Ben is in as I hear her chuckle behind me.

"It's called a Jumperoo, I like to place babies in them when I answer the door or do any nappy changes. I know they're safe then and won't hurt themselves or cause mischief," she explains.

I look at the Jumperoo thingy and smile at how much Ben is laughing away and jumping around. He looks happy, content and doesn't look like he has missed me at all. A fleeting sadness passes through me, but I soon shake it off. He needs this, the stable environment and to be in caring hands.

"Hey baby boy, you missed me?" I ask him. Ben looks at me with a big smile on his face before grabbing a toy and putting it straight in his mouth. Looks like I wasn't missed that much. I turn to see Charlie staring at me, she has such fondness in her eyes, and a warm smile. She really is beautiful and seems to have a good heart.

"How's he been?" I ask. Charlie snaps out her daze and looks at me.

"He has been amazing and is just the cutest little thing ever, you have done an amazing job with him."

At that compliment a massive smile covers my face. I do worry in case he is missing out on having a caring mum, but I know he is loved by all my family.

"Thank you so much, I'm so pleased he's been okay."

"You don't have to thank me, I always mean what I say," she says while placing a hand on my arm. The same tingles go up my arm again, only this time Charlie doesn't move her hand.

We just stand and stare for what seems like forever. Holly suddenly starts crying and it breaks us from the spell we seem to be under. Charlie quickly turns to her daughter to see that a tower of bricks has fallen over and being a typical two-year-old, Holly is upset by this. I chuckle thinking I have the lovely terrible twos still to come.

"Oh, Holly you're such a drama queen," Charlie says laughing. Picking her daughter up, she gives her a big cuddle to calm her down. I turn to pick Ben up out the Jumperoo and struggle to get his legs out. He's still bouncing away, as I try with all my might to get him out. I hear Charlie laughing so hard at me, as I try and figure how to get him out of this stupid thing. She puts Holly down and comes over, amusement still in her eyes. She takes over, quickly gets him out and hands him to me. Our hands brush, and this time Charlie quickly pulls away, a pink blush covering her cheeks. She is so adorable. We stand there entranced with each other. I have the sudden urge to grab her and just pull her into my arms, but I know she would freak out. It's too soon and she wouldn't want to jeopardize her job.

"Right little man let's get you home and sorted to go to Auntie Julie's later," I say, making it easier on her. I thank Charlie again and make sure all is set for him starting full-time on Monday. Leaving Charlie's house, I head home and put Ben down for a nap, while I sort his stuff out ready for this evening. I can't wait to go out tonight.

After dropping Ben off at Julie's, myself and Mike make our way into town. We're heading to a new bar that opened a few weeks ago, apparently its good. I don't care, as long as it serves beer, I'm happy.

Walking into the bar I get a good feel of the place. It has a modern touch, with booths lining one side of the room. High tables and stools covering the other side, with a dance floor situated in the middle. The bar is situated the whole length of the back wall. It's not too busy yet as it's still early, so myself and Mike make our way to the bar for a drink. After getting our drinks we find a free booth and take a seat. I scan the room, people watching, but not much is happening yet. Maybe it'll get busier a little later on.

"How was Ben then today with his childminder?" Mike asks.

"Yeah good, he was happily jumping away when I turned up. He was in this kind of big bouncy thing; it had all these toys around it as well." I state.

"Oh, you mean a Jumperoo? Me and Julie thought about one of them for Daniel, but they're so expensive," he tells me.

"Yeah that's it, it was fab. He seemed to love it, bouncing away."

Glancing around the room again I notice a blonde by the bar. There is something familiar about her, but I can't see her face yet. Still staring away, the blonde turns around, and it's then I lock eyes with Charlie. Fuck me sideways, she's looking hot as hell. A shy smile graces her gorgeous face, I can't look away from her. Something is pulling me towards her. I'm knocked from my staring contest with Charlie, when I hear my brother speak.

"Who the hell is that hot, little number?" he asks. I know I shouldn't be angry, but hearing him speak about her like that, has my blood boiling and me wanting to smack him one. I have no claim over her whatsoever. For Christ sake… she is my son's childminder, that's something I must keep reminding myself of.

I turn to my brother and try keeping my cool.

"That's Charlie, Ben's childminder," I try to explain calmly. Mike looks at me with his mouth wide open.

"That's the childminder? Fucking hell bro, she is smoking."

I look to Charlie again and ignore his comment. She is hot, but I can't go there. I can't risk her not been able to have Ben. Charlie keeps glancing over, she doesn't think I notice her doing so, but god I do. How can you not notice her? She is dressed in a tight red off the shoulder top, the tightest pair of black shorts, paired with the sexiest pair of fuck-me heels. She glances across, sees me staring at her again and her face blushes bright red. The sudden urge to be near her comes over me. Without thinking too much about it, I get up from my seat and stride across to her. Her eyes widen when she sees me approaching. Walking right up to her, I can see her more clearly, she has the lightest amount of makeup on and she just looks flawless.

"Hey," I say looking right into her eyes.

"Hey you."

"You look lovely" I say looking her up and down… I notice her check me out and then lick her lips. God what I wouldn't do to be able to kiss her right now. No, I can't have these thoughts, she is off limits.

"You here on your own?" she asks looking around.

"No, I am here with my brother." I tell her. Her friends stand to the side, just watching us with amusement in their eyes.

"Oh my god, I'm sorry this is Kelly, and this is Georgia," she tells me. Both girls look at me with knowing smirks on their faces.

"How you are doing?" I ask turning my attention back to Charlie. "Can I get you a drink?"

"Err, I am okay thank you, Kelly's just got one," she tells me. Suddenly my brother is by my side, I'd forgot I had left him just sat at the table.

"Hey ladies, I am Mike. This twat's brother," he says chuckling while pointing at me. "Would you ladies like to join us at our table?" Mike asks them.

Before I have chance to object, both of Charlie's friends shout yes, while dragging Charlie with them to the table. Sitting down, I'm somehow forced to sit next to her. I can't make up my mind if this is a good idea or not. Once we're all seated, Charlie places her bag in between us and her hand brushes my leg, her head snaps up and she looks at me. I know she feels this thing between us. I'm torn from either wanting to grab her, kiss the fuck out of her and running in the opposite direction. I've got to dampen down my feelings for her, I really do. Charlie shifts in her seat and we look across to Mike, who is talking away to her friends.

"You excited for Ben's first birthday on Sunday?" I hear Charlie say, turning to look at her, she really is gorgeous.

"Yeah, I am, not that he will understand what is happening, but I'm definitely looking forward to spoiling him for the day," I tell her. She has a big smile on her face… before I can stop myself, I ask her, "Hey if you're not busy on Sunday you're more than welcome to come and join in the fun with Holly." She looks torn on what to do. "No pressure," I say trying to reassure her…

"Do you know what? I'd love too," she answers.

I can't help the smile that crosses my face… I feel like an excited teenager who just got his first date. Yet this isn't a date, nope, I've to remember that.

"You can meet all the family just in case they ever come collect Ben, but it should always be me." I say this to convince myself that she is coming for any other reason other than I just want her there. There's just something about this woman that pulls me to her, she has such a natural beauty.

Thinking about my ex-wife I realise I never really did love her… I think I was more in love with the idea of having a wife, having a family. Molly hasn't been in touch once since we left, not one call or visit. Doubt Ben will get any communication from her for his birthday, but it's fine he will have enough love from my family and now Charlie.

"Excuse me," Charlie suddenly says… "I need the loo.".

Getting up I watch her walk away, my eyes going down to her sexy arse. Sitting down I fidget in my seat. I look across to Mike and see him smirking at me, he knows where my heads at. I am fighting not to go to the toilets and kissing the hell out of Charlie. My need for her is so strong. Thinking fuck it all, I get up and make my way over to the toilets. Just as I get there Charlie comes out. Not looking where she is going, she walks straight in my chest… my arms go around her to keep her from falling backwards. Her head comes up and I lock eyes with hers. Our lips are so close it wouldn't take much to kiss her right now.

"Oh, sorry I didn't see you there," she says, I see the pink blush cover her cheeks. Charlie steps back and I let go of her.

"We best go back to everyone." She says turning away.

Sighing in defeat, I nod my head and head back to the table with her.

We spend the rest of evening drinking and chatting. I've had the best night; I don't want it to end. I want don't want to say goodbye to Charlie and go home alone. I look to Charlie and find her staring at me, my breath catches in my throat at how beautiful she is. I swallow down the lump in my throat and try to find words to speak… I swear I am like a clueless teenager; I think laughing to myself. Charlie looks at me funny, wondering why I am laughing…

"Is there something on my face?" she quizzes me.

"No babe, nothing there."

Fuck, where did babe come from… I look to her again and she has a small smile on her face, a pink blush covers her gorgeous face and her eyes fill with lust… How I would love to just grab her right now and just hold her. I feel movement next to me, and noticed she has itched her way closer to me, with her hand resting on the seat next me… I glance down and have the strongest urge to hold her hand, to feel the warmth of it in mine. I move my hand and rest it next to hers. Charlie looks down at them and her little fingers brushes mine. Oh, fuck this, I grab her hand in mine and lace our fingers together. Her hand fits perfectly in mine and it's like we're meant to do this. Her skin is so soft, and I start wondering what the rest of her body would feel like. About how she would feel under me while I caress and worship her... before sliding in her and having her scream my name. I shake my head; I can't keep having these thoughts. I have only known her a few weeks, but there is honestly something about her that I'm drawn to.

The night draws on and before I know it, it's time to make a move home.

"Well I think it's time to call it a night." I hear Mike say, reading my exact thoughts. Charlie quickly pulls her hand away and I sigh at the loss of it. I stand up and move out the booth, holding my hand for Charlie to help her up, she glances at it before placing her hand in mine. I notice Mike and Charlie's friends staring at us, all with grins on their faces. We make a move to leave and walk Charlie out with my hand on the small of her back. I'm loving the smallest contact I have with her. The girls head on over to catch a taxi, a line already forming there.

"We will make sure you get in a taxi before we leave. There's no way I wasn't making sure you didn't get one safely."

With a smile Charlie thanks us.

"Thanks for a lovely evening," I hear Kelly say.

"Yes, it's been fab," Georgia agrees with her.

"Have you enjoyed yourself Charlie?" I ask her. With a small smile she nods her head

"Yes, I have loved every minute, thank you," she says.

A taxi pulls up and Kelly and Georgia climb in, I look at Charlie and place my hand on hers. Leaning down I place a kiss on her cheek, leaving my mouth there for longer than I know I should.

"See you Sunday, come over any time after lunch." I tell her.

She nods her head before turning to climb in the taxi. I stand there staring, watching the taxi drive away…

"You're completely fucked bro," I hear Mike say.

Nodding, I totally agree with him.

Chapter Seven

Charlie

Oh, my god. I am royally screwed. Sitting here in the taxi

going home, Kelly and Georgia stare at me with shit eating grins on their faces. Oh, they can fuck right off, smug cows.

"Come on say it, I know you both want too."

"What that you have the biggest crush on your new parent, who by the way is hot as fuck," Kelly tells me.

Groaning, I place my face in my hands.

"What the hell am I going to do?" I ask them both.

"Look babe, you of all people deserve some happiness in your life. I just don't want to see you get hurt that's all. He really does seem a lovely guy though." Georgia tells me.

My head is completely fucked up. Seeing him tonight dressed in a gorgeous pair of fitted black jeans and white button-down shirt. I swear I nearly come in my pants at the sight of him. He is beyond sexy and in any other life I would be all over him, but he is a parent of a child I will be caring for. Oh, I can't believe I agreed to go to his son's birthday party on Sunday. I wanted to laugh at him trying to justify why he asked me, I could see the lust in his eyes, it probably mirrored mine.

We arrive at Georgia's house first, reaching across she gives me a big hug and whispers in my ear.

"Go with your heart, it will lead you correctly."

Nodding at her, she climbs out and we watch her go into her house. Kelly is next to be dropped off, I've not far to go as I live literally around the corner from her.

"Watching you tonight I've never seen your eyes light up like they did when Lucas was with us. As Georgia said… go with your heart babe," she tells me.

I watch Kelly go into her house and then the taxi drops me off. Making my way inside I head straight to bed.

I go about my nightly routine of taking my makeup off, when suddenly my phone beeps from the side of the bed. Walking back into my bedroom I pick my phone up and notice it's a message from Lucas. I stare at the phone in shock, I don't dare look at what he's said. Why would he message me this late after only seeing him not long ago? Plucking up the courage I open the message app.

Lucas: I wanted to wish you a good night.

My heart rate picks up and I feel butterflies in my stomach. I swear this guy is going to be my undoing. I best respond to him.

Me: Goodnight Lucas, hope you have a good sleep. Thanks for tonight, I had the best night and look forward to seeing you on Sunday for Ben's birthday.

Oh god maybe I said too much, maybe I should have kept it short and sweet. My brain starts working overtime now, I start overthinking what I should have texted him. My phone beeps alerting me to another one.

Lucas: You looked gorgeous tonight, but you look gorgeous all the time.

Oh my god, he's flirting with me. This guy has me feeling all sorts of things.

Me: Thank you, you looked pretty good yourself.

Lucas: Wow, just good? I would say I looked damn amazing lol

Flirty Lucas is fun, I think to myself, but do I really want to lead him on? Deciding to just go with the flow I message him back.

Me: Well I would say more like hot, lol

Lucas: Are you flirting with me Miss James? I wish I was with you right now.

I sit staring at the phone for what feels like the longest time ever, but I think it was just a matter of minutes. I can feel my whole-body heating up. I know I am going to be seriously getting wet if we carry on like this. I bet if I looked in the mirror now, I would have stupidest smile on my face. Realising I haven't responded yet, I make quick work of replying.

Me: Oh yeah you wouldn't want to see me now, my hair is all a mess and I am about to put on some very questionable pyjamas lol.

Lucas: Believe me when I say, the pyjamas wouldn't be on for very long.

Oh, my fucking god. What is this man doing to me? Not knowing how to reply I decide to make myself more comfortable and get out my clothes. I'm just undressing when my phone beeps again... picking up the phone I read the message.

Lucas: You've gone quiet on me.

Standing here completely naked I crawl on the bed and forget the pyjamas. Getting myself comfy I reply.

Me: Now who is flirting Mr Jenson? Well the pyjamas are not on... yet lol.

Lucas: Charlie your killing me here, you have no idea how much I want to be there with you right now. To hold you, feel you in my arms.

Me: I want that too, but I need to stay professional, but god it's so hard.

Lucas: Believe me when I say it's very hard right now.

Fuck me that has got me so turned on right now… I can feel the ache building up between my legs. I know for a fact if I felt myself now, I would be soaked.

Me: Lucas what you doing to me? I never talk like this to a parent… and I've never been this turned on by a parent before.

Luca: Your turned on? Now there's a sexy thought, I bet your all wet aren't you…

Oh lord… this guy can talk dirty.

Me: What would you say if I said yes, I was wet… your making me want to get my BOB out!

Fucking hell, I can't believe I have just said that to him. He makes me lose my bloody mind. My thoughts keep drifting back to this evening, and the way he looked. I wanted to run my hands all over him.

He's gone quiet on me and I don't hear anymore from him. Oh god what if I've scared him away? I shouldn't have said what I did in the last message, he must think I'm a right nutcase. Suddenly I hear the doorbell go. Who the hell is that at this time of night? I throw on some sleep shorts and top and creep downstairs. I really don't want to open the door, I leave all the lights off, maybe whoever is there will go away. Suddenly my phone beeps, looking at the screen I see a message from Lucas.

Lucas: Open the door beautiful.

What the fuck. Lucas is at my door… I stand there in shock.

Lucas: Come on Charlie, I know your there, open the door beautiful.

Walking to the door I unlock it and open it, no sooner do I have it open and I am pushed back against the wall and his lips are on me. Fuck me this man can kiss. The kiss turns hotter, I feel his tongue at my mouth demanding entrance, opening my mouth, our tongues dance together. We only stop when we need to come up for air. His hands come to my face and he holds my cheek.

"You have no idea how long I have wanted to do that." I stand there speechless, not knowing what to say. "You're quiet babe."

"Erm, yeah, wow."

He looks at me with a smile on his face, grabs my hand and leads me through the house where he stops at the stairs

"Which is your bedroom babe?"

"Erm upstairs third door."

Leading me up the stairs I suddenly start having a panic attack, Lucas seems to sense this. What am I doing? He is the parent of a child I care for.

"Don't overthink this babe, we're grown adults and it's just us here."

Nodding my head, we walk into the bedroom and he leads me to the bed. My heart feels like it's going to explode out my chest at any moment. He stands in front of me and moves his hands up my arms, goose bumps break out all over me and he notices.

"You have no idea how gorgeous you are, do you?" He says as his hands move from my arms to my waist. Ever so slowly he moves them up, going under my top and I feel him skim my breast. My nipples instantly pucker. I have never been so turned on in my whole life. He grabs my hand and suddenly places it on his jeans covered cock. My god he is hard as steel, my reaction must tell him what I am thinking.

"You see how hard you make me?" He questions me.

I swear he is going to turn me to mush. His hands move back to my waist, then moves them slowly up again, this time he takes my top with it. He throws it on the floor and stands back to admire me. The way he is looking at me, with such hunger in his eyes, it makes me feel so wanted. I go to cover myself up, before I can do it, he grabs my hands.

"No, you are stunning Charlie, don't cover yourself up."

"I am so scared Lucas" I admit to him. "What if we fuck this up, I can't risk my job."

Looking at me he cups my face with both hands.

"Charlie, I have never felt like this before, not even with Ben's mum, there is something here. Tell me you feel it too?"

Nodding my head, I whisper, "Yes I do."

With that said, he crashes his lips to mine. Opening for him, our tongues tangle. I will say it again, this man, he can kiss. Breaking away, he peppers kisses down my neck and over my shoulder. Moving across he takes one of my nipples in his mouth. Tipping my head back I let out a groan, at the same time his hand comes up and caress the other breast. My whole body is alive right now, the feeling of him on my breast is amazing. Goose bumps covers my body as he sucks the nipple in his mouth.

"Lucas please" I beg. Not actually knowing what I am begging for.

"What do you want baby?" he asks, looking up at me.

"You, I need you." I state.

Chapter Eight

Lucas

I know I shouldn't be here. I know she probably feels like she is breaking all her rules, but god I can't stay away from her. Seeing her tonight dressed sexy as fuck, has left me with such a hard-on. While texting her earlier all I wanted to do was get my cock out and release all the tension I had built up, but I know it wouldn't be enough. Seeing her now standing here almost naked, I have never seen anything hotter in my life. Her tits are fucking amazing.

I lower myself down to my knees and pull her shorts down, she is now standing there completely naked. Fuck me, wow, I'm lost for words on how incredible she is.

I sense her wanting to cover up, but she is stunning. Her body is mine to worship, and worship is what I plan to do. Standing up, I pick her up and her legs instantly wrap round me. Kissing her again, I lower her on to the bed and step back. I could stand here all day just staring at her.

"Fuck me Charlie, you're gorgeous."

She smiles back at me; all be it very shyly. I pull my top over my head and throw it to the floor; next I remove my jeans and my cock springs out. I hear her gasp when she sees me. Now I know I am not massive in size, but I certainly didn't do bad in that department. I grab a condom from my pocket and throw it on the bed. Crawling up the bed I lay myself over her and bring my lips to hers in a soft, sensual kiss. Moving down her body peppering kisses as I go along. I feel her moving under me, trying to find the release she desperately needs. Going over her flat stomach, I place a soft kiss on the scar left over from what I presume is a caesarean. Looking up briefly at her, I place my mouth just over her pussy.

"I need to taste you baby, please say I can." Noticing a slight nod from her, I suck her clit right into my mouth.

"Oh, my, god, Lucas," I hear her say.

She tastes just like heaven, all sweet tasting. I continue to suck on her clit, at the same time pushing a finger in side her.

"Lucas please," she begs.

What the woman wants the woman gets, speeding up my licks, I insert another finger in and I start to feel her walls tightening. I can feel that she is about to come. Adding another finger seems to do the trick. Her whole back arches and she screams out. Fuck, that is the hottest thing I have seen, watching her fall apart from my mouth and fingers. Slowing down, I make my way up to her and kiss her, I want her to taste how amazing she tastes.

"Fuck Charlie, I need to be inside you right now."

Not waiting for a reply, I roll the condom on and place myself at her entrance, I look to her to make sure she wants this.

"Please Lucas now.".

With that said, I slam into her and she screams out. My god she is so tight and wet. I start moving in and out of her, grabbing behind her knees and bring her legs up, so I can hit that spot inside her. I hear her moan, so must have hit the right place. Speeding up I know this won't last long, fuck she feels amazing wrapped round my cock. It's like she is made for me. I start to feel her walls getting tighter around me.

"I can feel you baby; I know you're going to come."

"Yes, oh god yes… Lucas fuck, yes," she screams.

"Charlie come with me baby," I state.

I start thrusting harder and suddenly she is screaming my name as she comes all over my cock. That sets off my own orgasm and I follow her too. I flop down by the side of her, making sure I don't crush her. She is laying there with the most *'I've just been fucked look,'* and she looks bloody gorgeous with it. I know without a doubt; I am falling for this girl. Just one thing though, am I ready for it?

I pull myself away from her gorgeous body and make my way to the bathroom. I clean up and come back with a wash cloth and proceed to clean her up. Charlie jumps a mile at the coldness of the cloth and I try to hide my smirk, but I know she has seen it. Throwing the cloth on the floor, I lay back on the bed and pull her body to me.

"You okay?" I ask her.

She turns to look up to me and I can see the war raging in her eyes, looking like she is having a battle with herself. She pulls her eyebrows together and you can see her lost in thought at what has just happened. Her hands wringing together.

"Talk to me baby."

"That was amazing," she whispers.

Not what I was expecting her to say, but I will go with it.

"It was baby, I have wanted your body since the first time I laid eyes on you."

"Where do we go from here? I'm supposed to caring for Ben from Monday," she states, clearly she is upset because of what can happen.

"Now I've had you baby, I can't let you go," I tell her.

I see the shock on her face at what I have just said to her.

"Look its late, let's get some sleep and I will take you for breakfast tomorrow. What time are you collecting Holly?" I ask.

"She's with my mum so no rush for me to go get her, Mum loves having her."

"Okay then that's settled, sleep now baby." I tell her while placing a kiss to the top of her head. I lay there for ages just listening to her breathing. Once I know she is asleep I feel myself relax even further. I feel so contented, like this is where I am supposed to be.

This woman has wormed her way into my heart in such a short space of time. I don't think I can let her go, not now I've had her.

It wasn't how I thought my life would go when I walked away from Molly. Breathing her in, I sigh and feel myself falling asleep with her gorgeous body wrapped round me.

Tomorrow is another day.

Chapter Nine

Charlie

My eyes start to flutter open and it takes me a moment to acclimatise to my surroundings. Turning my head, I see Lucas laying on his side facing me with his arm wrapped round me. I take a few moments to lay there and stare at him. He has the most gorgeous face, I love his smile the most, it really lights up his face. With his dark hair and his gorgeous five o'clock shadow, I just want to run my hand over it. I can't believe I had sex with him last night. I'm not going to lie it was amazing, I've never felt anything like I did last night. Just thinking about it I can feel myself getting turned on again.

It seems I am in a constant state of arousal whenever I'm with him. Lifting the sheet slightly, I peek at his magnificent cock, man what he can do with that. Feeling brave, I shuffle down the bed and take his cock in my hand. I can feel it getting harder straight away. Without thinking too much about it, I take his cock in my mouth and start moving up and down, working him at the same time as my hand.

"Holy fuck Charlie," I hear him say. I feel his hands come to my head and start guiding me along. I glance a peek up at him and see the hunger in his eyes.

"Fuck Charlie, your mouth on my cock is fucking amazing."

I start speeding up at the groans and moans coming from him. Suddenly I am pulled from his mouth and spun flat on the bed.

"I am not coming in the gorgeous mouth baby, I need that pussy of yours," he states.

"Well what are you waiting for then?" I say, unsure where all this braveness has come from. I hear him grab a condom, roll it on and seconds later he is slamming into me.

"Oh God," I scream…

"No baby not God, but pretty close," he says.

He starts moving again and I can feel myself building to the release I so desperately need. All a suddenly I am flipped over, my arse pulled up and he is slamming back in once more.

"Now that's a fucking gorgeous sight," I hear him say just before his hand comes down with a smack on my arse cheek.

"Oh, fucking Christ," I scream.

"You like that baby?" he says.

"Oh god yes, Lucas please." I swear I have never begged this much before in sex. Lucas spanks me again and that's all it takes for my orgasm to explode.

"Oh, fucking yes, Lucas, yes."

I feel Lucas start to swell so know his orgasm is not far behind. He slams into me a couple more times before he is coming once again inside me. Flopping down on the bed, I bring Lucas down with me.

"Fuck baby, you can wake me up like that any day," he says.

I lay there with a big smile on my face feeling completely satisfied now.

After getting up, we both shower and it has to be the most sensual shower I've ever had. Lucas spends a long time washing my body and hair. He makes me want him all over again. We get out get dressed, Lucas walks up to me and places his hands on my hips, I have to look up to him since he is about a foot taller than me.

"Let me take you breakfast?" he asks.

"Okay, I would love to."

"I need to go home and change first, if that's okay?"

Nodding, we then walk downstairs, and I grab my shoes and bag. We walk out the house and I lock the door behind me. I am about to get in my car when he takes my hand and walks me to his.

"I will drop you back baby." he states. Holding the door open for me, I climb in, he shuts the door then walks around to the driver's side and gets in.

After going back to Lucas's so he can change, we make our way to the local pub that is open for breakfast. Finding a table and we sit down. I select a menu and beginning looking at it. I can feel his eyes on me, so I glance up see him staring at me. Reaching over he grabs my hand, lacing his fingers with mine.

We sit like that while we order our food and wait for our drinks. Breakfast goes smoothly, and we spend the time talking about everything. Lucas asks me more about why I became a childminder and I ask him about his job.

All too soon it's time for me to go get Holly and for him to get Ben. I find myself slightly disappointed and not wanting this morning to end. I've enjoyed his company, a lot more than I thought I would. Lucas drops me back home, so I can collect my car. Climbing out he comes around to me, grabs my hips and pulls me flush against him.

"I can't wait to see you tomorrow. I will text you later okay." He bends down and places his lips against mine. I can only nod, as this man can make me lose the power of speech.

Parting ways I walk to my car, climb in and head to mums. Life certainly has a way of throwing you off. I was adamant I didn't need a man in my life. Now I am not so sure.

I reach my mums house and go straight in. I don't get very far as Holly comes charging towards me knocking me flat on my backside.

"Hey baby girl, you've missed me, haven't you?"

Dropping lots of sloppy wet kisses all over her, she wriggles out my grasp laughing. I've missed this girl.

I know she doesn't know her dad, and yeah maybe I should have told him, but that bastard doesn't deserve the love of this sweet girl. She is bloody lucky she is here, after the shit he put me through. I am glad I'm out that relationship. I couldn't allow him in her life, after he beat me when pregnant. I knew I had to get away. I don't want her knowing that monster, he doesn't deserve the love from her.

"Hey mum, how's she been?" I ask, getting up from the floor.

"She's been a darling as always sweetie, you know I love having her. You need to start going out more and enjoy your life while you're still young."

Wow that's me told. Holly is sitting on the floor building with some bricks she has here. Sitting down with her I start building a tower, to which she knocks down straight away and laughs about it.

"You want a drink sweetie?" mum asks.

"Yes, please mum, you got any Pepsi in?"

She will have, as she knows I hate tea or coffee. Mum goes off into the kitchen to make the drinks. Looking at Holly, I can't help, but smile. She is the most precious thing in my life. She is the one good thing I ever did, well that and my job. I am amazing at it; I laugh to myself.

"Here sweetie," mum says, handing me my drink.

Holly gets up and makes her way over to mum to get her drinks beaker. She can drink out a normal cup now, but we only allow her to at the table. Looking up to mum, she is looking at me weird.

"What's up mum? You have a weird face on you."

"I don't know, there's something is different about you I can't put my finger on… You eating okay? You're not on one of these silly diets, are you?" she asks me.

"No, you know me, I love my food too much," I say laughing. I have no idea what she is on about at all.

"Are you dating anyone?" mum asks.

What the fuck. Has the woman got magic powers or something? I haven't been with a guy for over two years, yet the minute I'm with someone she asks me if I am dating. Mothers.

Putting on my best *'lie'* face, because come on I can't exactly tell her I slept with a childminding client, can I?

"No mum don't be silly, when do I ever have the time?"

"As I have said, you need to get out more. I'll start having my gorgeous granddaughter more for you. Start living a life darling. I want you happy and I haven't seen you happy for a long time. Well until you met those two lovely girls you work with, but I don't know, you seem even more happy now, so whatever it is, keep doing it."

I feel tears prick my eyes. I blink them back, I can't cry, not in front of Holly. I get up and walk over to mum.

"I love you mum," I say hugging her hard.

"I love you too sweetie, so much."

We break away and I turn to Holly.

"Right baby girl, shall we go to the park for a bit?"

"Park, park," she says back. I take that as yes then.

Getting all her stuff together, I hug mum again, thanking her for last night and well yeah, just everything really and then I get Holly in the car. We head to the park for a bit, before heading home for dinner.

By the end of the day I am shattered. Last night and well this morning is now starting to catch up on me. After getting Holly to bed, I decide an early night is needed and make my way up. I haven't heard from Lucas all day, I guess he is busy getting sorted for Ben's first birthday tomorrow.

I really shouldn't be missing him this much, but I am. Once sorted for bed, I get all comfy and turn the TV on. I end up falling asleep with it on.

My night is filled with a sexy dark-haired man.

As I said before, I am fucked.

Chapter Ten

Lucas

Today's the day, I woke up thinking I can't believe my baby boy is one today. Where the hell has this last year gone?

So much has changed in the last year. Some things not being good. Other things like meeting Charlie have been fantastic. After dropping her off yesterday, the whole day just went so fast. It felt like I didn't have five minutes to stop. I wanted to message her last night, but by the time I had finished wrapping presents and decorating the living room, it was too late.

Hearing Ben on the baby monitor, I make my way out the bed and into his room.

"Morning my gorgeous birthday boy," I say to him. His little face lights up every time he sees me in the morning, he really does make my day. Picking him up I hold him close.

"Looks like your Mummy isn't going to be seeing you for your birthday, since I have heard nothing from her. Come on Ben, let's go have some breakfast before Grandma, Grandad and Uncle Mike and everyone are here to spoil you."

Making my way downstairs I place Ben in his highchair and switch the coffee machine on. Picking up my phone I message Charlie.

Me: Morning baby

Hearing the coffee machine doing its thing, I get Ben his breakfast sorted and some water to drink. This kid doesn't really like milk much, only prefers to drink it for bed. Making my coffee I sit down and feed Ben his Weetabix.

One thing I can say about him, he is a good little eater. Once finished, I get us both dressed and sorted, then go back downstairs. I know my family will be here very soon, they are just excited as I am. My phone vibrates on the kitchen side, so I place Ben on the floor to play and go grab it. Looking at the phone I see its Charlie.

Charlie: Hey you. How's it going? Missed your message last night.

Me: I am sorry baby, by time I stopped it was late and didn't want to disturb you. I can't wait to see you later.

Charlie: Yeah about today, can we not let on to anyone we're together please?

What the fuck. Why would she ask that? Then I remember her been worried about her job, and what people would think or say.

Me: If that's what you want baby, although I would love to tell everyone. lol

Charlie: Thank you Lucas, I just don't want anyone to judge me.

Me: Baby no-one will judge you. I think my brother already knows how I feel about you anyway.

Charlie: Just for me, for now, I would like your family to see me as professional and not some slapper who jumps on every guy she meets.

Me: Right first thing first. Don't ever and mean don't ever call yourself a slapper again. Secondly my family wouldn't think that, but for you baby, yes, we can keep it quiet.

Charlie: Thank you. What time you want me and Holly there again?

Me: Come around about one'ish if that's okay? My family will be turning up very soon, so that gives them time with Ben before you come babe.

Charlie: Okay that's fine. I will leave you to get on, give Ben a birthday hug from me and I will see you soon. I can't wait. I miss you.

Me: Miss you too baby, see you later.

Placing the phone down, I go over to Ben and pick him up.

"Hey little man, Charlie sends a big birthday hug your way," I tell him hugging him hard. "She has me under a spell, just you wait until next week little man, you'll be the same," I say laughing.

Suddenly the doorbell goes. "That will be Grandma, Grandad and the rest." Making my way to the door I open it to a very excited Mother.

"There's my gorgeous birthday boy," she says smothering him with kisses. Ben starts giggling away and it's one of the best sounds around. Mum takes him out my arms and walks into the living room with him. I let the rest of the family come in, eyeing all the bags of presents as they carry them in. I groan to myself, as I told them all not to go overboard, since he has no idea what today is. Where the hell am, I going to put it all?

Walking into the living room my parents have already started opening presents with Ben. I laugh to myself since I think they're all more excited than me. Ben sits on my mum's knee not having a clue what the hell is going on but loving all the attention he is getting.

We spend the morning opening a few presents before Ben gets ratty, so I take him upstairs to bed for his nap.

While he is sleeping, I set about making food for everyone with mums help.

"Charlie, Ben's new childminder is coming around soon. I invited her to his birthday party, so she could have a chance to meet you all. You know just in case any of you have to collect him for me," I tell her. She looks at me with side eyes.

"It will be nice to meet her; I have heard a lot about her from your brother."

Oh fuck. Right play it cool, she won't figure anything out. Oh, who am I kidding it's my mother, of course she will.

"Don't know what you mean mum, there's not much to say really. She is Ben's new childminder nothing more." I say trying to sound convincing, but I know straight away I have failed.

"Lucas Jenson, you don't you fool me, I see the sparkle in your eyes when you talk about her. Your brother has already explained."

See I can't bloody hide fuck all from her. I groan and place my head in my hands. Charlie didn't want anyone knowing about us yet, what the fuck do I do now? Mum walks up to me and grabs my hands.

"What's up Lucas? You know we all just want you happy," she states.

"I am happy mum, just Charlie is concerned how you will all see her if you knew about us? She wants you to see her as professional, please don't let on just yet that you know," I plead.

"My darling boy of course we all can. I can't wait to meet her. We haven't seen that smile on your face for a long time."

I bend down, hug my mum, and kiss the top of her head. I honestly couldn't wish for better parents. They have been there for me through everything since I found out I was going to be a dad.

Suddenly the doorbell goes, and I pull away from mum to go answer it. Opening the door, I am greeted by the most stunning woman ever, Charlie stands there with her daughter in her arms, fast asleep.

"Hey sorry I am bit early, she fell asleep. I didn't want to just sit in the car looking like a looney and there was no point going home," she tells me.

Bending down while no-one can see me, I place a soft kiss to her lips. I feel her moan against my mouth and my dick instantly hardens at the sound of it.

"I am glad you're here baby," I tell her while pulling away. "Come on in and meet the family"

I take her hand and lead her in to the house, but I feel her pull her hand away before we reach the living room. I know it shouldn't bother me, we agreed to this, but I can't help it. I just want to take her in my arms and tell everyone. Walking in the living room, I introduce Charlie to everyone.

"Hey this is Charlie, Ben's childminder and her daughter Holly. This is my Dad Frank, my mum Lorraine, Mike you already know and his kids Daniel who's two as well, his older daughter Jasmine who is six and his wife Julie."

Charlie waves to everyone

"Hi everyone, it's nice to meet you all, sorry about Holly, she is fast asleep," she says laughing. "Can I put her down anywhere, she is kind of heavy?" she asks with a smile on her face.

"Of course, here." I lead her into the other room with a small sofa next to the dining table.

"Will she be okay on here?" I ask her.

"Yes, this is perfect, she will probably wake soon anyway," she says. Charlie lays her down and I reach for the blanket on the back of the sofa and lay it over Holly. Looking up, Charlie is smiling at me. Without a second thought I grab her hips and pull her flush to me

"You look sexy as fuck right now baby." I lean down and capture her lips, stroking my tongue along the seam of them, she opens to me and I caress her tongue with mine. Fuck this woman is going to be my undoing. Breaking away I reach down and reposition myself. Charlie sees this and giggles away. Fuck, if I thought Ben's giggle was cute, fuck me hearing Charlie is the hottest thing ever. Smoothing a piece of hair behind her ear, I just want to carry on holding her.

"Come on baby let's go and see everyone. We will leave the door wide open and keep checking her. Ben will be awake very soon as well."

Walking back into the living room I notice I was right about Ben; mum sits on the floor with him playing away with some of his new toys.

"Hey little man, did you wake up or did naughty Grandma wake you up herself?" I say laughing looking at mum, who just shrugs her shoulders not really caring.

"Oh, I have a present in the car for Ben, do you mind if I go get it quickly before Holly wakes up?" Charlie asks.

"Of course, go right ahead," I say.

Charlie walks out the room and I hear the front door open. Suddenly Charlie is back again, with someone standing behind her.

"Lucas there is someone here for you."

I turn towards Charlie and notice the one person I wish to god to never see again.

"What the fuck are you doing here?" I growl at my ex-wife... well soon to be ex-wife.

"Well that's no way to greet me is it husband dear, I am here for my son's birthday," she exclaims.

"Not a fucking chance, you haven't seen or even asked about Ben in the last two months. You didn't want fuck all to do with him."

I can feel the anger building inside of me. My fists are clenched at the side of me and I am shaking. I'm just raging inside. I notice Charlie still stood at the door not knowing what to do. Molly notices me look at Charlie, then turns and glares at her.

"So, who is your little lady friend here Lucas?"

"None of your fucking business," I shout.

Ben starts screaming behind me, then Holly from the other room. Fuck, I didn't mean to scare the kids. Mike walks up behind me and places a hand on my shoulder.

"Me and Julie will take the kids into the garden away from all this mate. They don't need to be hearing all the shouting and swearing," he tells me. I nod because I know he's right. I never swear in front of any of the kids, but this fucking woman brings out the worst in me. Mike picks up Ben from my mum, then walks to the door, just as Charlie comes back with Holly in her arms.

"You want us to take her in the garden?" Mike asks her.

"Erm, she might not go, I will come out with you and settle her, if that's okay?"

"Of course, come on." Mike takes everyone to go play in the garden on the big play equipment I built out there. While I stare at the bitch in front of me.

"Right, now they're out the way, what the fuck do you really want?" I ask her. She just stands there with a smile on her face. What the hell did I ever see in her?

"Now, now, baby, that's no way to treat the mother of your child."

I have never hit a woman in my life and never will but fuck if she doesn't make me want to.

"So, who's the blonde bimbo you keep eyeing up?" she asks me just as Charlie walks back into the room. I see a flash of hurt pass her eyes, but it's quickly gone as she squares her shoulders and stands tall.

"Hi. I am Charlie James and you are?" she says in a confident tone.

God I bloody love this woman.

Wait, what?

Where the fuck did that come from?

I know I have strong feelings for her, but love?

Pushing them thoughts aside, because now is not the time to be thinking about that. I notice Molly just give Charlie a look of disgust, fucking bitch. Charlie doesn't seem to rise to it, instead walks and stands next to me. Mum also walks up and stands with me

"Look I think you need to leave; you want to see Ben then we will get the solicitors in place and set it up," my mother tells her.

I love my family.

"Oh, fuck this shit I can't be arsed," Molly says then turns and storms out the house, slamming the door behind her. I let out a breath I didn't even know I was holding. Charlie turns to me and places a hand on my arm

"Are you okay?" she asks with such concern in her eyes.

Turning I hold her hip with one of my hands and nod.

"Yeah, I am good, thank you for that," I tell her. I hear my mum cough behind me, Charlie jumps away forgetting that my parents were stood there. I chuckle to myself because, I know that they all know, but she doesn't think that. Turning to mum I notice both her and dad with big smirks on their faces. I shake my head at them both.

"We're going to go out to your brother and the kids, take five minutes, both of you," dad says while patting my arm.

They both walk out, and I turn back to Charlie, pull her to me and just hold her.

I now know now without a shadow of a doubt; I love this woman.

Chapter Eleven

Charlie

I stand here in his arms and I can feel his heart beating against his chest. When I realised it was his ex-wife who had turned up, I didn't know what to do. I felt like I shouldn't be there... There's no doubt that she is pretty. but god is she a grade 'A' bitch. If she hadn't had left when she did, I don't think I would have been held responsible for my actions. I wanted to punch her when I heard her call me a blonde bimbo. I'll give you blonde bimbo, bitch. I look up to Lucas and see the serious expression on his face

"You okay?" I ask while placing a hand on his cheek, he looks down at me and nods, then bends and places a kiss on my forehead.

"Come on let's go see the others and make the best of what's left of Ben's birthday."

He grabs my hand and we walk out, I should drop the hand, but I know for a fact from just looking at his parents faces they know about us. No point in hiding it now.

The rest of the afternoon goes by smoothly and Ben is spoilt rotten. You can see how much this family means to each other and I love how much attention Ben gets. That little boy is just gorgeous and deserves everything the world can offer him. I can't wait to start looking after him tomorrow. I decide it is time to leave when I see Holly yawning her head off again. Even with all the food and cake she has had, she's still flagging.

"I am going to take Holly home if that's okay?" I ask.

"Of course, babe, I will walk you both out."

I say goodbye to everyone, pick up Holly and follow Lucas out. I strap Holly in her car seat, shut the door and turn to Lucas, he cups my face, leans in, and kisses me hard.

"I will miss you. I'll see you tomorrow morning, let me know when you get home," he tells me.

Nodding my answer, I climb in the car and head home. I know my feelings for him are getting stronger, I just don't know handle it all.

I wake the next morning full of excitement for the day ahead. I have everything ready for Ben to start, the Jumperoo is out again for him, I know he likes it. Its brilliant in keeping young children entertained when sorting lunches or answering the door. I also have the highchair near my table all ready for him. Lucky for me I am only feeding him lunch. He gets dropped after breakfast and collected before dinner. George and Lilly are already here since they're the first to be dropped off, the doorbell goes, and I know that will be Ben.

"Right kids that will be Ben the new baby, please stay here and play nicely. I will be back in a sec." I instruct them both. Both nod in agreement, but I'm not sure if they are both listening to me.

Walking away I go to the front door and open it. A gasp falls from my lips when I see Lucas stood there looking absolutely fuckable. Man, what I wouldn't do to jump him right now. My gaze travels all the way up his body until I meet his eyes, and I notice the smirk on his face. The fucker knows I was checking him out again.

"Like what you see babe?" he says grinning. A blush covers my cheeks and I turn my attention to Ben, ignoring Lucas and his sexy smile.

"Hey there, my beautiful boy, missed you lots," I say to him. He responds with little giggles, which is the most amazing sound in the world. This little boy is already worming his way into my heart and it's the first day. I stretch my arms to him and he happily comes across to me for a cuddle. Lucas comes in to the porch area after I step back and places his bag on Ben's peg.

"Anything major to tell me about him today?" I ask Lucas as I look up to him, but suddenly without warning, he bends down and places his lips softly on mine. It's only a small peck to the lips, but I know I am going to feeling it all day. I suddenly hear my name been shouted from the living room and remember the kids are in there, I really need to get to them.

"Nope nothing to tell you, he is fine, and his dummy is in the front pocket," he tells me.

"Thank you, I best get back to the kids," I say.

We say our goodbyes; I close the door and take Ben into the living room to the other kids. Who yet again have trashed the place. Why? Seriously why today? I place Ben in the Jumperoo, so I can try and sort the room out. Welcome to Monday morning.

The day passes by quickly and Ben is a delight to have. He has been so lovely and oh my god the cuddles this kid gives... I can see him been spoilt by me. He has definitely got a hold on me. Its nearly time for Ben to be collected, all other kids have surprisingly have been collected early today. I love it when that happens, early finish for me. I am just finishing up placing some toys in the boxes while Ben and Holly are playing with the baby tablet on the floor next to me. When I hear the doorbell, I go to answer the door and grab Ben on the way.

"Come on sweetie, that will be daddy. Stay here Holly, mummy will be right back," I tell her.

I open the door to Lucas, and Ben's face lights up at the sight of his dad. I smile at their father and son bond; it really melts my heart. Lucas comes straight in, takes Ben out my arms and holds him close.

"There is my gorgeous little man, have you had a good day with Charlie?" He looks at me for confirmation.

"He has been a delight to have, he is so relaxed for a baby. You have done a fab job with him," I say honestly. Lucas smiles wide at my compliment, then steps forward and looks down at me.

"You got any kids left?" he asks me.

Only managing to shake my head, because yet again I'm lost for words, with him being so close to me.

"Good I can do this," he says while pinning me against the wall and kicking the front door shut. His lips crush against mine while trying not to squash Ben in between us. My head becomes so lightheaded and my legs become weak. It's a good job I'm flat against the wall, otherwise I don't think I would have stayed stood up. We break away when we both need air to breath. He strokes the backs of his fingers down my cheek.

"Thanks for today, glad he was good."

"You're welcome," I reply in breathy breaths.

"I best get him home for dinner. I will see you in morning." he says giving me another quick peck on the lips. He collects Ben's bag and opens the door to leave.

"I will text you later," he says as he makes his way down the garden path. Waving bye to them both, I close the door behind me and lean against it. I am seriously falling hard for this man.

After dinner me and Holly settle to watch the bedtime hour on her TV channel. I suddenly hear my phone beep from the kitchen where it's charging. Leaving Holly where she is, I make my way to the kitchen and pick it up, I notice it's a message from Georgia.

Georgia: Hey Fanny, what you up to?

Me: Not a lot, why? Everything okay?

Georgia: Good I am on my way round; I need out this house before I kill him.

Oh, dear what's the bastard done now? I fucking hate her husband and just wish she would leave him.

Me: Okay babe, I will put Holly to bed and I have wine in the fridge. Just come in.

Georgia: See you soon fanny.

I laugh at her name for me, it always cracks me up.

"Come on Holly, time for bed."

Picking her up I take her upstairs and start getting her ready. I hear Georgia come in downstairs. Once Holly is in bed, I make my way downstairs and find Georgia in the living room with a glass of wine in her hand and one poured for me.

"How was Ben today?" she asks me.

"All good, but never mind me, what's up?"

Georgia lays her head back on the sofa and closes her eyes. When she opens them again, I can see the tears shinning back at me.

"I fucking hate him Charlie. I really do. Every time he drinks, it's like he sets out wanting an argument with me. I can't do anything right around him."

"Why don't you leave him?" I ask her.

"I can't, he has threatened to take everything, the house, car, the lot. I can't lose the house, I need my job," she states angrily.

I seriously want to go and punch this fucker. I see the tears start to fall down her gorgeous face. So, I reach over, pull her close for a hug and let her get it all out. My anger starts to boil about the fact that he makes her feel this way. She pulls away and wipes her eyes with the back of her hands.

"Sorry, I am a crying mess."

"Please you know I always have your back babe, why don't you stay here tonight?"

"No, it's okay, it will only cause more problems. I don't want all the questions on where I'm staying for the night. Plus, I need to be back for the kids in morning."

I only nod my reply, because I know it's pointless trying to change her mind. We spend the next hour talking and helping her feel calmer before she decides to leave. I hug her tight whispering in her ear.

"Remember I am always here; I will see you tomorrow babe."

Nodding she heads out the door and walks home. I close the door and clean up, before deciding on an early night. Climbing into bed and getting comfy I decide to call Lucas. I noticed earlier he had texted, but I didn't want to ignore Georgia, so left his text. The phone rings a couple of times before he answers.

"Hey beautiful, what do I owe this pleasure?"

"Sorry it's late, I missed your text earlier because Georgia was here and thought it would be easier to call you back."

"Well it's always good to hear your voice."

I smile at his words.

"What you're doing now"? he asks.

"I am lying in bed, what about you?"

"Lying in bed also, but now I am picturing you in bed. I hope your naked," he asks, I just know that he has a smirk on his face.

"Nope, not naked, sorry," I laugh down the phone.

"You have to spoil my fantasy, don't you?" He says laughing. I can't help the smile that graces my face.

"I think you need to be naked right now, maybe we should switch this to video call," he says in a meaningful tone. Suddenly my phone switches to Lucas doing video call, I answer the call and his smiling face greets me.

"Now, there is my sexy girl."

I can't help the warm feelings I get from him calling me this, he makes me feel so cherished. No-one has ever made me feel the way he does.

"So why aren't you naked?" he asks me again.

"Because you're talking to me," I laugh.

"Come on baby I want to see that gorgeous body of yours."

Suddenly I'm feeling nervous, I have never done anything like this in my life. I don't even know if I can. Lucas must sense my feelings.

"Hey baby it's just me and you remember, no-one else is around."

Feeling slightly braver, I start to remove my top using my one free hand and end up all in a tangle. I can hear Lucas laughing so hard on the phone at me. Once I have managed to get my top off, I glare at him, but soon soften when I see the heat in his eyes as he stares at my chest. I fight my instincts to cover myself up, he makes me feel beautiful.

"Fuck baby, I love your tits."

His words hit me right between my legs and I feel myself getting wet.

"You're getting wet aren't you baby? I can see it in your sexy face. Now loose the shorts."

Placing the phone down on the bed I do as he says. I pick the phone back up and look back into his eyes.

"Don't think this is fair though somehow, you're still fully clothed."

Suddenly I am staring at his ceiling, while I assume, he is stripping. He returns completely naked and I can't help the gasp that leaves me when I see him. Fuck he is hot.

"I know what you're thinking baby and believe me it's making me rock hard."

His hand reaches down, and I know he is palming himself.

"Touch yourself for me," he demands

I hesitate slightly, but start to caress and pull at my nipples. I am soaked and can feel myself building up to an orgasm without even having touched myself between my legs. I normally can never get myself off without a vibrator. My breathing gets heavier and I know Lucas is feeling the same.

"I want to see you play with yourself baby, put them sweet fingers on that sexy pussy."

Moving my hand down my body, my fingers brush my clit and I arch my back...

"That's it baby, fuck that tight hole."

His dirty words make me rub my clit faster, I insert a finger and I know it won't be long before I am falling apart. He has me right on the edge and we haven't even done much, and he isn't even here.

"You nearly there baby? I am so close and want to come with you." Lucas says in panting breaths.

"Yes, oh fuck Lucas, I'm close... I am going to come, Lucas, oh fuck," I scream out as I have one of the most intense orgasms I've had. Not long after, I hear Lucas grunt his release. I look at the screen which I still can't fucking believe I am still holding and see Lucas staring back at me. The look on his face is what I could only describe as love... No, that can't be right, love no way. We haven't known each other long enough, but I know my own feelings and I am falling big for this man.

"Fuck Charlie that was sexiest thing I have ever seen," he tells me, and I end up with a pink blush covering my face. Lucas sees this and chuckles. We talk for a few minutes more before I start yawning away.

Lucas notices, "You're tired"

"Yes," I admit.

"Okay gorgeous I will let you sleep. I'll see you in morning."

Saying goodnight, we end the call and I place my phone on charge next me and switch my side light off. I fall asleep with a smile on my face and butterflies dancing around, with a feeling of love inside.

By Wednesday I seem to be in a constant state of arousal whenever Lucas is around. Every time I open the door to him my heart beats faster. I just want to grab him and have my wicked way with him. I know tonight, I've got to have him. I've arranged for him to collect Ben a bit later than the other children and plan to cook him dinner.

At the end of the day, once all the kids have gone, I set about sorting dinner out. Making sure that Holly and Ben are settled in the living room; I go to the kitchen.

Twenty minutes the doorbell goes, and I know that will be Lucas, my heart rate picks up straight away. God what this man does to me. Opening the door, I'm left breathless, he truly is gorgeous. Instantly I'm so turned on. Lucas stands there smirking at me, knowing where my thoughts have gone. Cocky git.

We have dinner and get the kids sorted for bed. I'm desperate for this man to be inside me. Dragging him straight to the bedroom, I push him on the bed where he falls flat laughing. Putting my phone on my portable speaker, I select Christina Aguilera's Dirty, to play and start to strip my clothes in a sexy way. God. I've never done this is my life, but the look on Lucas's face allows me to carry on and give him show.

"Fuck Charlie, you're hot," he says while rubbing his hand over his cock. I'm so turned on its unreal. Once I've removed all my clothes, I walk over to Lucas making sure to add an extra sway to my hips.

Dropping to my knees between his legs, I move my hands up his thighs and get to the button of his jeans. My hand brushes his cock and I hear him suck in a breath. Popping the buttons open, he lifts his arse to allow me to pull them down his legs, freeing his magnificent cock. My mouth waters just looking at it. I grab him in my hand and start teasing him. I can feel him losing control already just from the expression on his face. I can see he wants to grab me and just take me.

"Charlie babe, you carry on like that and I'll be coming in your hand in a minute," he says through gritted teeth.

Taking pity on him, I stand and allow him to remove the rest of his clothes. He grabs my hips and pulls me flush to him.

"You are beautiful," he says.

Smiling I press my lips to his, what starts of as a small kiss, soon turns more heated. Spinning me around, Lucas pushes me so I'm leaning over the bed.

"God what a view," I hear him say.

I hear him rip open a condom and rolls it on, lines himself up with me and thrusts inside. My god, he feels so good. Lucas picks up speed, and I feel him trying to hold back his release. He reaches round and flicks my clit…

"Come for me Charlie."

That's all it takes, and I exploded around his cock. A couple of thrusts later and he comes himself. I collapse on the bed bringing Lucas down with me.

"God, I needed that," I whisper, trying to catch my breath. I hear Lucas chuckling behind me.

After getting cleaned up, we lay together in bed and just enjoying each other's company.

The following day flies by and before I know it, it's Friday. I'm so ready for the weekend. As much as I love my job, I do love lazy Sundays, chilling with my girl in our pyjamas.

I have just put Ben and Holly down for a nap and I'm just tidying up the lunch dishes when the doorbell suddenly goes. Frowning, because I am not expecting anyone, I make my way over to answer the door. When I open it, the person stood there is one I wasn't expecting. Ben's mum, Lucas's ex-wife stands there with a smirk on her face. God, I hate this woman and would love to knock that smirk right off her face.

"Can I help you?" I ask her.

"I want my son," she bites.

Well lady you're in for a fucking shock because you aren't getting him, I think to myself.

"I'm sorry, but that can't happen."

"Look bitch that's my son in there and I'm allowed to see him"

"Well I am truly sorry, but you aren't setting foot in this house," I state in a forceful tone. Fucking rude cow, who the hell does she thinking she is speaking too?

"Ben is asleep at the moment, and even if he was awake, I'm not permitted to let you see him. The contract I have is not with you, but his father. So, no, he isn't going anywhere," I say in a calmed tone.

In a more hushed tone, I add, "Now can you kindly piss off my property before I have to call the police."

With that said, I slam the door in her face and walk in to the kitchen. Banging starts on the front door. Not wanting the kids woken up, I have no choice but to open the door again. Not before I quickly shoot off a text to Lucas, letting him know what has happened.

Me: Hey Lucas, I just want to let you know, your bitch of an ex-wife is here demanding to take Ben. Over my dead fucking body is she having him. If you see me on the news for murder, it's because I have killed her lol.

Placing my phone down, I return to the front door and yank it open.

"Will you fucking stop banging before you wake not only Ben, but my fucking daughter," I say in a hushed, but firm tone. "I have told you; you aren't coming in here. He is asleep, and his contract is between me and father. I can only allow contact with those that are named on the contract."

"Who the fuck do you think you are? You're just a babysitter."

Oh no, she didn't just fucking call me a babysitter, that's the worst thing to call me. Fucking babysitter my arse.

"Now listen here lady, get off my property and get lost. You're not getting Ben, under any circumstances, he is my responsibility at this time, not yours."

The look that Molly is currently giving me reminds me of the saying *'if looks could kill.'* I just want to laugh at her, who the hell does she think she is?

"This isn't fucking worth it," she says before turning around and storming off. I so want to shoot back a witty remark, but I hold my breath. I close the door and laugh. Stupid fucking woman… don't mess with me, you won't win.

Picking up my phone I notice I have a couple of missed calls from Lucas. Oh, crap, he's probably going to be in a right flap now. I try ringing but get no answer. I shoot him a text informing all is okay now and she has gone. I start to tidy up again thinking one of the kids will be awake soon, when the doorbell goes again.

"If that's her back, I swear to god I will fucking kill her" I whisper to myself, while walking to the door.

"What now," I ask in a tone that says not to mess with me, while opening the door. Lucas just stands there, but not for long, as he suddenly grabs me, pins me to the wall behind me, kicks the door shut with his foot and holds my face in his hands.

"Please tell me you're okay and Ben is still here?" he asks with such concern on his face. I bring my hands to his face, and nod.

"Yes, I'm fine, that bitch won't get past me. She won't get Ben. I'd have to be dead first before she got anywhere near him," I say to reassure him.

I don't get chance to say anything else, because his lips crush to mine. He pours his feelings right into that kiss. He pulls back slightly and rests his forehead against mine.

"Where are the kids?" he asks.

"They're having a nap."

"Good" he says bending and lifting me up from under my knees, I wrap my legs around his waist as he walks us into the living room. Sitting down with me on his lap, his lips brush mine in a soft kiss. Holding my face in his hands, he looks in my eyes.

"Thank you for today, I hope she didn't hurt you in anyway."

"Nah she doesn't stand a chance with me; she won't get Ben from me. Not without your consent," I tell him honestly.

His face softens, and he looks at me like I am his whole world. He stares into my eyes and I can see love shinning back at me. He places a hand against my cheek with such softness.

"I need you baby, I need to be inside you," he tells me.

Nodding, he suddenly lifts me and lays me down on the carpet. He starts removing his clothes and his impressive cock springs out before me. Leaning up, I kiss the tip and I hear him moan. Grabbing hold of him I take him in my mouth and use my hand to cup his balls.

"Fuck Charlie, your mouth is so good on my cock."

He holds my head and threads his fingers in my hair. I speed up and start sucking his cock. The noises coming from him, tells me that he likes what I'm doing. Suddenly he pulls out my mouth and looks down at me.

"I need to be inside you baby when I come," he says before removing my clothes and forcing me to lay back down. He starts kissing up my thighs and I shiver in anticipation.

"This will have to be quick baby," he tells me, I nod my agreement and he grabs a condom, rolls it on and lines himself up at my entrance. Looking deep into my eyes he thrusts balls deep inside me.

"Fuck," I think to myself, or maybe I said that out loud as I hear him chuckle. He starts moving again and straight away I can feel my release building.

"Fuck Charlie, your pussy is gripping my cock." he grinds out. I can see him fighting with himself so not to lose control. He really starts fucking me and I know it won't be long before I am coming all around him. Suddenly I am flipped over, and he thrusts back into me from behind. He pulls my arse up, so I am basically on all fours.

A loud smack echo's through the room as a sting hits my arse.

"Fucking hell," I scream as I thrust my arse back to him. He smacks me again and that's all it takes; within seconds I am coming all round his cock.

"Fuck Charlie," he says as he starts pounding me even harder. Seconds later I feel him start to swell before he comes inside me. We fall on the carpet. both us spent. He holds me close and my heart feels like it's beating out of my chest. Laying here now I know without a doubt I love this man.

He holds my heart and I am not sure I want him to let go.

Chapter Twelve

Lucas

I stare at this amazing woman laid next to me and I know

I love her. What she did today just proves it. She stood up for Ben, that's all I have ever wanted for him was someone to love him and protect him. I don't want to move from this spot, but we both hear the soft cries of Holly over the baby monitor.

"The kids are awake," Charlie tells me on a chuckle because she knows I really don't want to move. I pull away from her and dispose of the condom, and we both get dressed.

"Come up stairs with me to get the kids please," she asks me.

We make our way upstairs to Holly's bedroom where she is sat on her little toddler bed with her stuffed toys looking ridiculously cute. Ben is stood up in the travel cot in the corner of the room. I walk over to him and pick him up.

"Hey little man, you have a good sleep?" I ask him, while looking at Charlie, who is sat at the side of Holly's bed, playing with her and her stuffed toys. I get down on the floor next to her and place Ben on my lap. Holly hands him a stuffed tiger which he happily takes and starts chewing on the ear. Both me and Charlie just laugh. Holly really does seem to love Ben; she is always passing him toys and will cuddle him whenever he cries. Sitting here I start to see what I am missing. What I long for… A family. I take Charlie's hand and thread my fingers through hers. Looking deep in her eyes I say the three words I know I mean.

"I love you."

She looks at me and I see the love shining back at me.

"I love you too," she tells me honestly. I lean down and kiss her. This right here is what I want. I want her in my life and don't want to let her go. I need to sort my ex-wife out and quick.

"Come on its Friday lets go out for dinner, all of us. Do you have any kids after school?" I ask her.

"No, they've all been collected by their parents for a change," she says.

We get up and make our way downstairs. Charlie packs a bag for Holly and even makes sure that she has stuff in there for Ben. Seeing her do this makes me love her even more. Molly would never have done anything like that. She wouldn't have even thought to do it.

"Shall we take my car; I have seats in there for them?" Charlie asks looking at me.

"That's absolutely fine babe."

Making our way out to the car we strap the kids in and head out for dinner.

We arrive at my favourite restaurant Frankie and Benny's, I don't know how she knew, as I don't think I have ever told her.

"How did you know this is my favourite place" I ask her. She looks at me confused

"I didn't this is my favourite place," she says smiling.

Leaning over the centre console, I pull her to me and kiss her lips.

"I absolutely love you," I tell her again.

"Love you too," she says back.

I don't think I will ever get sick of hearing that. We walk in to the restaurant and are shown to a table. Placing the kids in the highchairs, making sure their strapped in and we take our seats, and start looking at the menu.

The evening is spent having a lovely meal and the kids are amazing and well behaved. We leave the restaurant and walk hand in hand back to the car. I can't keep my hands off her, even if it's just holding her hand. I have to be touching her in some way. We reach the car and strap the kids in. I open the door for Charlie and she climbs in giving me a sexy smile in return. I walk round to the passenger side and climb in. We make our way back to hers, as I need to collect my car.

I don't want to leave her though; all I want to do is crawl into bed with her and make love to her all night. I want to hold her close and never let her go. We park up and I go to climb out, but she grabs my arm and pulls me back.

"Erm, Lucas, will you, I mean if you want, you can stay with me tonight."

I smile at her words; she is just too damn cute when she becomes all shy. Reaching over to her, I hold her face and kiss her softly.

"I'm not leaving you; I want to hold you in my arms all night long. I want to wake up with you in morning. I want to have a breakfast with all of us together. I love you," I tell her.

A big smile adorns her face telling me she likes what I said.

"I love you too" she says.

We get out of the car and head inside. The kids are getting tired and I know Ben will want a bottle soon.

"Do you have a spare bottle?" I ask her.

She goes over to the cupboard and grabs it, lucky for me I always pack more powder in his bag for him just in case it's needed. I don't fancy the idea of having to go home.

"I have some spare clothes here in my box that Ben can wear for bed," Charlie informs me.

This woman has everything you could possibly think of because of her job. We get the kids ready for bed and then tuck them both in, leaving the night light on, then head downstairs with the baby monitor in my hand.

"Do you want a drink?" she asks me, but I just pull her to me and kiss the shit out of her.

"I want your hot body Charlie. I want to fuck you so hard that you won't be able to walk straight for days," I tell her.

I know she is turned on, because she starts rubbing her thighs together to try and ease the tension I know is building. Taking her hand, I lead her back up the stairs, forgetting about the drink she offered. Walking into her bedroom, I close the door and place the baby monitor on the side table. I walk over to her and gently lift her top over her head. She has a sexy lace, baby pink bra on and god does it make her tits look fucking gorgeous. I reach down, undo her jeans, and peel them down her gorgeous legs. Removing her shoes, I pull her jeans off the rest of the way, leaving her stood there in just her lacy underwear. Fuck me, she is just amazing.

"Fuck Charlie, you're gorgeous, there are so many things that I want to do this gorgeous body right now."

"Well do it already," she tells me with an attitude. I chuckle and start removing my own clothes.

"On the bed Charlie now," I tell her forcefully.

She crawls onto the bed, making sure to add a little sway to her hips at the same time, which makes me I growl at her. I take a condom out my pocket, lay it on the bed next to her and crawl up her body, peppering kisses as I go along. She starts squirming underneath me, so I place a hand on her stomach to hold her down. I reach her pussy and I know this is where she wants the attention. I just hold my face close to her and she can feel me breathing where she wants me the most. Getting back up I remove her underwear very slowly, taking the time to tease her.

"Lucas please," she begs me.

I take pity on her, remove her knickers, then thrust a finger inside her. The moan that leaves her tells me she is enjoying this. Leaning down I take her clit in my mouth and suck it gently. Her back starts to arch and her juices are coating my finger, fuck me she is so wet for me. I thrust another finger in and start building up speed. Fucking her hard with my fingers, all the while I suck and flick her clit with my tongue.

"Fuck, harder Lucas," she moans.

I insert another finger and her walls get tighter round them, I know she's getting close.

"Come baby, I want to feel you on my fingers and tongue," I tell her.

That does it and she scream out in pleasure, as she comes all over my fingers. Watching her fall apart is the hottest thing ever. I remove my fingers, bring them to my mouth and suck them, her eyes widen in shock.

"Sweet tasting," I smirk at her. I grab the condom, begin rolling it on and make my way up her body. She looks fucking gorgeous laying here for me.

"You're mine baby, don't ever forget that."

"Yes, I am all yours," she replies in a breathless tone.

I line myself up and in one quick movement I thrust myself deep inside her.

"Fuck your pussy is so tight baby."

I start moving and she matches my every move. It's like where one together. I can feel the love pouring between us as I fuck her slowly, I don't want to rush this, I want to feel her all around me.

"Fuck, your cock is so good." She says as she takes what I'm giving her.

"I know baby, it fits perfectly in your wet pussy."

I don't want to ever leave her; her body is made for me. We mould perfectly together.

"Please Lucas," she begs.

I comply with her demands and start moving faster. I can feel her release building again and know she is going to explode all over me. I can feel my own orgasm building, but I don't want to cum before her.

"Are you close baby? Come with me," I tell her.

She nods, because it seems that she has lost the power of speech. I fuck her harder when I feel her walls tighten around my cock, then she screams out as her orgasm takes over. Feeling her explode sets of my own release and I shoot inside her, her own orgasm milking me for everything I have got. I flop to bed beside her, so I don't crush her and pull her close me.

"I love you so much Charlie," I say honestly, she turns her face and looks straight at me. Holding my face, she kisses my nose.

"I love you too," she says back to me.

We stay like that for a few minutes before I get up and dispose of the condom. I make my way to the bathroom and come back with a cloth and clean her up. She looks fucking adorable laying there with a *'I've just been fucked look.'*

Climbing back into bed I pull her to me, her back to my front, and kiss her shoulder. We both lay there for ages chatting away with the TV on in the background. I feel Charlie yawn next to me and I know she's getting tired.

"Sleep baby," I tell her.

Her breathing evens out and I know she is asleep. I fall asleep myself knowing I have the most gorgeous woman in my arms and I'm not letting her go.

Waking the next morning and I turn to see Charlie laying on her front, her hair fans around her and she looks perfect. Placing a little kiss to her shoulder I get up and make my way to the bathroom. I use the loo, brush my teeth then make my way back to Charlie. I grab my phone quickly to check I haven't missed anything when I see a message from Molly. I groan to myself, I'd rather not hear from her, but know I must.

Molly: We need to talk now. I know you're with that bitch babysitter.

Fuck this woman gets my back up. I look to Charlie sleeping and decide to deal with this now rather than later. I throw on some clothes and make my way downstairs. I press call on her name and wait for her to answer. I know it's early, but I don't care, this woman irritates me to no end.

"Hello Lucas."

God her voice even irritates me.

"What do you want?" I ask. I not going to be nice to her she doesn't deserve it.

"Well that's a nice greeting from you. We need to talk, I'm moving away."

My heart starts pounding at the thought of her wanting to take Ben from me. No, she wouldn't want him. She can't have him.

"What you mean you are moving, over my dead body are you taking Ben"

"Oh, calm your fucking tits, I don't want Ben," she states.

I release a breath I didn't even know I was holding.

"So, what do you want?" I ask her.

"Meet me today will you, I don't want to have this conversation on the fucking phone."

"Fine, I'll meet you in an hour at the coffee shop near my house."

Agreeing she hangs up and I stand there not knowing what to make of it all. I make my way upstairs to Charlie and the kids. I know they will be awake soon and I want to see if Charlie is okay with having Ben while I go and meet that bitch. I really don't want to take him with me. If she isn't able to have Ben, I am sure my mum will watch him for me. Sitting down on the edge of the bed, I trail my finger along her naked back.

"Charlie, baby, wake up".

She turns slightly and looks at me with a smile on her face.

She is so gorgeous.

"Morning," she says while stretching her body out. What I wouldn't do to just crawl back into bed with her and fuck her until she is screaming my name again.

"Morning beautiful, sorry to wake you, but I need to go meet Molly." I groan her name out. Charlie sits up straight at the sound of her name.

"Why you're meeting the devil woman?" she asks, making me laugh.

"Don't worry baby, she messaged me saying we needed to talk. I rang her, and she informed me she is moving away."

"She isn't taking Ben, nope over my dead fucking body. I won't allow her," she shouts out.

God, I love how protective she is over Ben.

"Hey, don't worry she isn't taking Ben, can you watch him for an hour while I go see what she wants?" I ask her.

"Of course, that's absolutely fine."

"Thank you," I say while kissing her. I say goodbye and make my way to meet the woman who I wish I would never see again.

I walk into the coffee shop and notice her sat in the corner. I take a good look at her and wonder to myself what I ever saw in her. Where Charlie is all natural, wears hardly any makeup, doesn't need to dress to impress. Molly has the fake nails, the bleached blonde hair… and just generally looks fake. I make my way over to her and sit down. She looks me up and down, but not in a nice way, you can see the scowl on her face.

"You look too fucking happy, is it that bitch babysitter making me you miserable?"

I grind my teeth in an attempt not to say a snide remark.

"Look, cut to the chase, what do you want?"

"I'm moving away."

"Yeah you said that, what's it got to do with me?" I'm already desperate to leave, this woman just gets my fucking back up by just being here. "The divorce is going through whatever you want take it up with my solicitor." I inform her.

"I told you calm your tits will you, I want twenty thousand pounds."

My mouth drops open in shock, she has got to be fucking kidding me.

"You're kidding right, you want more money?" My anger starts to build. "Deal with my solicitor." I tell her, angrily.

"Give me the money and you can keep Ben." she replies like it's just a business deal and not her son. I clench my fists, trying to fight the urge to punch something.

"This goes through my solicitor, but if I give you this money, you sign your rights away to Ben," I tell her.

"Fine if that's what you bloody want."

She looks at her nails, as if she's not even remotely bothered about Ben. This woman is impossible.

"Why in the hell did you come to Charlie's house if you don't care about Ben?" I ask her, wanting to know why she did it.

"That was to mess with you. Look we both know I am not his mother, never will be," she explains, she honestly has no maternal bones in her body.

"My solicitor will be in touch," I tell her. I get up and leave her sat there without saying another word. I make my way back to my car and get in. I call my solicitor and inform him about everything that has just happened, and he tells me he will get it all sorted.

I breathe a sigh of relief that she could be fully out of mine and Ben's life. She never wanted him and never will. No matter how much I tried to make her form a bond with him when he was born. It was never going to happen. Realising I did all I could, I put the key in the ignition and start the car.

I make my way back to the woman who I love with my whole heart and soul.

The woman who without a doubt I know loves Ben unconditionally will be there to protect him.

For the first time in a long time I can see happiness in my future, and that makes me smile.

Chapter Thirteen

Charlie

Six Months later.

Life has been a rollercoaster for the last six months; Lucas's divorce came through and Molly signed her rights away to Ben. Part of me felt bad for her, how could anyone not want this gorgeous little boy. He has captured my heart big time. Holly absolutely loves him to bits and protects him. She is definitely my mini me. Myself and Lucas are completely happy together and I wouldn't be without him now.

He officially moved in my house about two weeks ago. It made sense for him to move here since I have everything set up here for the kids. I still love my job and don't want to give up childminding. If it wasn't for this job, I would have never met Lucas.

The kids love each other so much. Holly is so protective of Ben and doesn't leave his side at all. It makes my heart burst with pride with how amazing she is with him.

Lucas's mum has offered to look after the kids this evening so we're going out for a rare meal together. I am looking forward to a few hours with just me and Lucas. I love the kids, but it's good to let my hair down every now and then. I am busy getting ready when Lucas comes into our room.

"Is you're mum here yet?" I ask him.

"Yeah she is downstairs," he walks over to me bends down and kisses the top of my head. I stand, and he looks at me, dragging his gaze all the way up my body. He makes me feel so wanted and so cherished. There is no doubt how much I love this man.

"You look stunning Charlie," he says. I smile, and a blush covers my cheeks. "Are you ready baby?"

"Yeah, let me grab my shoes," I say and walk to our wardrobe.

Walking downstairs, I make my way to the kids, kiss them goodnight, and say bye to Lorraine, thanking her for watching the kids. We head to our favourite restaurant again and sit down at a table. We order our food and Lucas takes my hand in his. We're sitting there chatting while we wait for our food to arrive, when suddenly Lucas lets go of my hand. Everything that happens next is such a blur.

"Charlie. I love you so much. You came in to my life when I didn't think I wanted it, but I needed it. The way you have loved and protected Ben is all what I wanted for him."

reaches into his pocket and brings out a small box. I gasp in shock when he gets down on one knee at the side of the table, while still holding my hand.

"Love me forever Charlie... Marry me?"

He opens the box and there sat nestled in the silk, is the most beautiful single diamond ring I have ever seen.

"Yes, yes, oh my god, yes," I say throwing myself at him and both of us ending up in a heap on the floor. Suddenly everyone is clapping around us. Lucas grabs my face and kisses me with everything he has. Taking my finger, he slips the ring on.

"I love you so much Charlie, you're mine forever," he says, and I know it is true.

When I thought I didn't need love again, this gorgeous and amazing man proved me wrong.

"I love you so much too," I say.

I know our life will be a happy one together. We've got each other, and we've got two amazing children who we love unconditionally and will protect forever more.

Getting up off the floor we sit back down at the table just as the food arrives. We sit and eat in a comfortable silence with both of us just looking up at each other. Nothing has to be said, we know how each other feels just by looking.

After we've eaten and paid the bill, we make our way back to the car and head home. The sexual tension between us is now starting to rise, we both feel it. Making our way indoors, Lorraine comes running straight to me, grabs my hand and squeals with happiness. I take it she already knew what Lucas had planned.

"Oh, I'm so happy for you both," she says with tears building in her eyes. I lean over and hug her. This lady has come to mean so much to me. We say goodbye and I head on up and check the kids, both are sleeping soundly. After kissing them both on the head, I make my way to the bathroom and start removing my makeup. Once finished I enter the bedroom and gasp in shock. Scattered all around the room are candles, burning bright. The room looks gorgeous and there laid on the bed is my future husband. Just saying that makes me smile. Getting undressed I go to the bed and crawl up to Lucas. Suddenly I'm flipped over so I'm on my back and Lucas just stares into my eyes.

"I love you Charlie."

As he says this, he pushes himself into me and starts to make love to me. It's not rushed, we just take our time. I know I love this man with my whole being. He holds my heart; my soul and I never want it back.

He came into my life when I didn't think I needed anyone, nor wanted it, but he worked his way into my heart and I couldn't be happier.

"I love you Lucas," as I say this, we both come together.

Spent from our lovemaking, Lucas holds me close, never letting me go.

Epilogue

Charlie
Three Years Later.

I stand and stare at myself in the mirror. Today is my wedding day and I am wearing a beautiful A-line white dress, with small thin straps, and a gorgeous lace back. It has a small train attached to the back as well. I decided I didn't want a veil; I chose just a small tiara instead. We planned to get married a year after we got engaged, but a surprise arrival in the shape of our son Samuel put a stopped to that.

Samuel is two years old now, and we wanted to wait until he was old enough to be part of the service.

He's the apple of his dad's eye and so much like his older brother, Ben, who is four and half now. The kids love Samuel and I honestly couldn't be happier.

Holly comes to stand next me looking gorgeous in her princess white dress with pink sash around the middle, it has small butterflies along the bottom as well and I love it. She's isn't far off six-years-old and is already starting to get an attitude. God help me when she hits her teenage years.

I look down to her and smile, she may have an attitude, and there are days where I get so angry with her, but I honestly couldn't be prouder of her. She protects her two brothers so much and I know as they grow up, she will be there to carry on protecting them.

"You ready beautiful?" I ask her.

She nods, and we go and grab our flowers and head on out to the room where the wedding is taking place. We chose a gorgeous old barn located on a beautiful farm not far from where we live. That has authentic wooden beams, decorated with flowers all over them.

Arriving at the doors Ben comes along dragging Samuel along with him. It's the first time I've seen them both dressed for today and straight away my eyes well up with tears.

"Now don't you go ruining your makeup young lady," my mum barks at me with a grin on her face. Bending down I hug both boys.

"I love you both," I tell them smiling.

"Right let's do this," I say standing up. The doors open, and the kids make their way down the aisle. Mum takes my arm and I look to her smiling.

"Thank you, mum," I say, trying not to cry again, god I'm an emotional wreck.

Looking to the front of the aisle I see Lucas; my eyes lock on to his and I know my heart is pulling me straight to him. The music starts to play, and mum and I start walking. All the time it's like everyone around me disappears and all I see is Lucas. Once I reach him, all I want to do is kiss the life out of him, he looks sexy as fuck in his black fitted suit. What fun I will have ripping that off him later. The smirk on his face tells me he knows where my thoughts have gone. His eyes roam down the length of me and I see the heat in his eyes. I know exactly what he's thinking.

"You look beautiful Charlie, what I would do to have you now," he whispers in my ear.

The wedding happens in a blur, all I want is to get to the part where I can kiss this man of mine. That part arrives and Lucas holds my face and it's like time stands still. His lips touch mine and I melt.

This man here is the reason I breath… him and these three kids are my life.

I never thought I would ever find my true love from doing my job, but life has a way of changing its course. My life is complete, and I couldn't be happier.

Lucas pulls back and stares in my eyes.

"I love you so much Mrs Jenson, now my life is complete," he says.

I look at him and blush. Staring into his eyes I say, "Lucas I have something to tell you… I'm pregnant."

Spinning me round on the spot in front of everyone, I can't help the smile on my face, I guess he is happy.

Our life is perfect. Me, Lucas, and our children.

We may have battled with our feelings in the beginning, but I wouldn't want my life any other way.

He holds my heart and soul and I don't ever want it back.

The End

T.A. Andrews

About The Author

Reading has always been a big love of mine, and when an idea come to me, I decided to give writing a go.

Living with my husband and son, and working from home, it has allowed me the flexibility to write.

In June 2018, my writing journey started.

At 39 years old, I am now enjoying writing my stories, all the while still being able to do a job I enjoy.

T.A. Andrews

Social Links

Facebook:
https://www.facebook.com/Author-TA-Andrews-406409503438903/

Instagram:
https://www.instagram.com/authortaandrews/

Readers Group:
https://www.facebook.com/groups/1451647198303999/

T.A. Andrews

Printed in Poland
by Amazon Fulfillment
Poland Sp. z o.o., Wrocław